VIRGIN DAIQUIRI

LOVE AFTER MIDNIGHT #2

ELISE FABER

SNARKY BOOKS FOR SNARKY MINDS

VIRGIN DAIQUIRI
BY ELISE FABER

VIRGIN DAIQUIRI
Copyright © 2020 Elise Faber
Print ISBN-13: 978-1-946140-66-1
Ebook ISBN-13: 978-1-946140-65-4
Cover Art by Jena Brignola

LOVE AFTER MIDNIGHT

Rum and Notes

Virgin Daiquiri

On The Rocks

ONE

Brent

I SMILED at Brooke and Kace, or rather, I smiled as Brooke settled in with her computer while Kace stared at her like she owned his heart.

Because she did.

Still, it was Christmas Eve, last call was done, the bar was empty and clean. Which meant, my duties were complete. It was time for me to go back to my rental and go to sleep.

Pathetic?

Maybe.

But I'd gotten used to being alone.

Better that way.

I waved to Kace and slipped quietly by Brooke, not wanting to disrupt her flow as she wrote the latest bestselling romance novel. Technically, I'd known her longer than Kace, and I still felt real guilt at not having kept in touch with her after her brother and my friend, Hayden, died. I should have looked after her better.

But the past was the past, and I, more than anyone, understood that it belonged there.

Sighing, I stretched my aching back—reason one I'd gotten out of the military—and walked away from the bar. I'd just reached the doorway to the hall when a tiny female crashed into me.

"Oof," I grunted, instinctively reaching out to steady her. "Easy there, darlin'."

She stiffened and pulled back. "I'm sorry," she said, and my gut clenched from the impact. Her voice was sweet summer peaches, warm honey dripping down fingers. It was the most intoxicating thing I'd ever heard. "I should have been more careful."

"You're fine, darlin'."

She nodded, lifting her hand to push her bangs from her face. It was trembling, as was her voice, when she went on. "I left my purse. I can't believe I was so stupid to—"

"What color was it?" I asked gently.

"Black with a gold zipper and chain."

I nodded. "I have it. Come on," I said. "I saw it left behind and put it in the office." I'd set it on Kace's desk earlier while on break.

Her relief was palpable. "Thank you so much. I swear, my whole life is in that bag."

"Your *whole* life?"

She smiled, and it was another punch to the gut. I had the distinct thought that I wanted to see that smile forever. *What?* Blinking away the crazy idea, I turned and led her down the hall, opening the door marked private and pointing to the desk.

Her hands came up and she clasped them to her chest.

"Oh, thank God."

"You come here often, darlin'?" I asked and mentally

winced at the words, which came out sounding like a lame pickup line.

"No," she said, fiddling with the neckline of her shirt, smoothing it out before bunching it up again. "I just moved to town."

"Ah. You going to come back in tomorrow?"

Her cheeks went a little pink. "Um. You guys are open on Christmas Day?"

Oh. Shit. Now I'd gone from lame to sounding like a total idiot. "Oh. Um. No, we're not. I . . . forgot."

"You forgot Christmas?" she asked, stepping forward to pick up her purse, head tilting to the side in an adorable fashion.

I shrugged. "No family here. Not a ton to celebrate."

"Oh."

And now I could add pathetic to the list.

But then she glanced up and I saw warmth in her gorgeous blue-green eyes. "You could come over to my house. I was going to cook and—"

The warmth in her eyes died.

Probably because my expression was coming across as shocked. Or maybe a little disbelieving. What kind of woman invited a strange man back to her house? Moreover, what kind of woman invited a strange *black* man to her house?

That had happened to me exactly . . . never.

"Never mind," she said, biting her lip, eyes dropping to the floor. "It was a stupid idea."

I huffed out a laugh.

"I'm *not* stupid," she snapped.

"Inviting strange men you don't know to your place for Christmas isn't exactly smart."

Those eyes shot up, and my breath froze in my lungs. Blue tinged with green. The ocean reflecting the hot summer sun. Pretty and delicate and somehow still strong.

Then she spoke again, and I couldn't keep the amusement out of my expression. "You're not a strange man," she said. "You're the man who saved my life by keeping my purse safe." Her chin came up, and that small show of spine was the third punch to my gut. "Serial killers don't rescue purses."

I snorted. "Whatever you say, darlin'."

A huff. "I'm new in town and don't have any family, and you seem nice, so I invited you for dinner." She tossed up her hands. "What exactly is the problem with that?"

"Because sweet little girls like you don't invite men like *me* places."

Her brows drew together. "Men like you?"

I rolled my eyes. "Men"—I pointed at my face—"like me."

She disappeared. I literally had no other word to describe it, but one second, she was all fire and the next, she was a blank slate.

"Girls like me," she repeated, and her voice was no longer sweet peaches and sticky honey. It was ice. "I see. Heaven forbid a *girl like me* ask out a handsome man because a *girl like me* should be at home knitting or collecting cats or darning my socks." She sighed and turned away. "Or at the very least, hanging her star on a man who fits her. Someone plain and dumpy and average-looking."

Um. What?

"You're far from average-looking, darlin'."

She winced like I'd punched her.

But I wasn't blowing smoke. This woman was small and curvy with delicate features. Her skin was all peaches and cream, her eyes a mix of blue and green, one I'd never seen before, and her blond hair was lush and thick, hanging in silky waves down her back. Too much sweet in a small package.

And too much sweet for me.

"I'm reading you loud and clear," she muttered, spinning for the door. "Don't need to hit below the belt. I'm going back to my empty house, back to my imaginary cats, and won't darken your doorstep again."

Fuck. Someone needed to save this woman from herself.

That someone couldn't be me.

But that still didn't stop me from snagging her arm and rotating her to face me. "You live near the city now. You have to be smart." Her lips parted again, probably to tell me she *was* smart, but I kept talking. "*Street* smart. You can't tell strange men you live alone *or* invite them back to your place."

"Fine," she said.

"Fine," I agreed.

But I didn't let her go.

Her eyes flicked over my shoulder, to the ceiling, and my gaze followed hers, half-expecting to see a giant spider dangling there.

Instead, I saw mistletoe.

I glanced back down. She licked her lips.

And suddenly, I knew she was thinking the same thing as me. Warm bodies pressed together, lips only inches apart, heat filling the space, and a kiss-inducing plant overhead.

"Mistletoe," she whispered and licked her lips again.

Just one taste.

I could give myself that.

I bent my head and slanted my mouth across hers.

TWO

Iris

SOFT LIPS.

That was the only thing I could think.

His mouth had been pulled so tight, his jaw clenched firmly enough that I'd noticed a tick just in front of his ear, but when his lips met mine, they were gentle.

A brush that stole my breath.

My lips parted.

And then . . . he kissed me.

It was almost chaste, his hands staying at his sides, not coming up to tug me against his body, even though I would have gladly plastered myself against him. And his tongue stayed in his own mouth.

At least until *my* tongue did something it had never done before.

Well, not without coaxing and forcing myself to work up the courage to make the move.

Anyway, this time I didn't need coaxing or courage or

shoring up my spine to make the leap. Almost without thinking, it slid free of my mouth, darting lightly against his lips.

The change was instant and electric.

Arms banded around my waist, yanked me flush against his chest, trapping my hands between us. But I didn't mind, not when it meant they were pressed against the hard muscles there, and I especially wasn't crying about being close enough to have the man's scent wafting up, surrounding me, soaking into my pores.

It was spicy and masculine, so much different than my own mix of floral and baby powder.

Not that I had a baby.

I just adored the smell of baby powder.

I hoped the man did, too.

My brows drew down, and I almost came out of the kiss with the realization that I didn't know the man whose lips were currently pressed to mine, but then his tongue chased my own back into my mouth, tangling and teasing and ramping chaste up to hot, and I forgot about the fact that this was only the fourth person I'd kissed.

Ever.

Ever.

Frank. My parents. And now . . . this man.

Oh, God—

I was kissing a man, and I didn't even know his name!

Panic swarmed me, and I yanked my head back, trying to shove out of his arms and completely unable to free myself.

"Let. Go," I said, panting and completely aware of the fact that it was from the kiss, and not because it had been bad. But because I was kissing a man I didn't know. I didn't kiss men. Hell, I was too shy to even *talk* to men.

But here I was, in a bar.

In a man's arms.

And I didn't know his name.

"You have to let me go," I said, wriggling in his hold, trying to free myself. I watched the beautiful man blink, deep pools of unfathomable dark eyes coming back into focus after a moment. "You don't know who you're kissing," I continued blithely. "You don't—"

His arms opened.

I stumbled back a step.

"I—" I shook my head. "I—"

"I shouldn't have done that," he said, voice placid, face expressionless, eyes over my shoulder. "Not with you." He pointed to the door. "You should go."

Slice.

Rejection.

I knew that feeling intimately, had felt it frequently.

So, I didn't cry or wither or let my face show how deeply that wounded. Instead, I bundled it up with the rest of the pain from my past and shoved it deep down. Then I bent to retrieve my purse, it somehow having fallen to the floor without me noticing.

Probably because even though I'd been kissing a stranger, the feel of his mouth, his lips, his tongue . . . were more incredible than anything I'd ever experienced with Frank.

I'd kissed just two men.

Not hard for the one in front of me to beat Frank.

Not only because Frank was a total jerk, but because Frank and I had been bumbling teenagers when we'd been together.

Sigh.

"Don't worry," I said, pushing Frank from my mind. "I'll go."

"Good."

The short, sharp syllable made my filter disappear.

Or at least, that was the only reason I could think for my

normally shy and locked-down nature to have poofed away like fairy dust, the next words out of my mouth being a total blurt.

"And I definitely won't come back and drool over you all night again," I snapped. "I certainly won't sit at the bar for three hours and hope that you notice me. Because I get it. Beautiful men like you aren't into dumpy, fat girls like me."

His eyes shot to mine, going wide, gorgeous lips parting, but I wasn't going to let him tell me to go again.

I spun for the door.

I was going to see myself out. I was going to forget about extending ridiculous invitations to dinner, about kissing gorgeous men whose names I didn't know.

I'd been humiliated enough for a lifetime.

Frank had seen to that.

Now *I'd* seen to that.

Lifting my chin, I reached for the handle.

Then found myself being hauled back against a strong, broad chest.

"You're beautiful. It's not you—"

I snorted, shoving at his arm. "Okay, let me stop you before you finish that *It's not you, it's me* nonsense." Another shove, which meant I managed to loosen his grip all of a millimeter before it banded tightly around my middle again. "I've got the picture. Let me flounce off with an ounce of my dignity intact, will you?"

"No."

Cool.

Let me start off by saying I didn't usually condone violence, but I'd been pushed to my limits, and this man, the one who'd given me the best kiss of my life—yes, it was only the best kiss of two total men, but I also didn't have to be an idiot who'd only kissed two men to know that it still had been a really good freaking kiss—was holding me firm, wasn't letting me escape my embarrassment—which had reached critical mass—and I snapped.

I tilted my chin down and bit him on the forearm.

Not lightly.

He cursed, arms falling open, and I shoved forward lurching for the door, grasping the handle and yanking it open.

The last thing I heard as I stumbled out of the office was the cursing cut off and his rumbling voice chase me down the hall as I fled.

"So, what time is dinner?"

I'd entered the bar chastising myself for being an idiot who left her purse behind, and I left that same bar, chastising myself for still being an idiot.

Albeit this time, one who'd left some of her dignity behind.

THREE

Brent

I GLANCED down at my arm, at the two perfect crescents of teeth marks, and felt my lips curve up.

I shouldn't be amused by the fact that the woman had just bitten me.

But, one, I'd had it coming.

And, two, I'd had it coming.

First, for kissing her. Even though she'd stood there under the mistletoe looking as sweet as a Christmas cookie—cheeks a little flushed, blue-green eyes darkening, lips parted, tongue darting out. She'd kissed me back.

But sweet girls like that didn't kiss me.

They were scared of me.

I was a big, black guy. I was built, and my default expression was scowl, especially when I had to haul some rowdy fucker out of the bar. Brooke even liked to tease that my resting bitch face was more powerful than hers.

Still, I'd had the bite more than coming, and not just because of the kiss.

But because I'd let her think that I hadn't wanted to kiss her.

Because I'd been warring with myself, thinking that I didn't deserve to have my hands on such a beautiful, sweet angel, my lips, my tongue—

And then the angel had shown me a slice of the devil.

With her teeth.

Hard enough to surprise, not hard enough to really hurt.

I glanced back down at my arm, saw the marks had already faded, then looked down the hall, the flash of her blond ponytail disappearing into the front room. I followed slowly, intending to lock the door behind her, but about halfway down the hall, I kicked something.

It clattered across the floor.

I looked down, saw it was a cell phone, then bent and picked it up, just as the beautiful angel-devil rounded the corner, muttering to herself about idiots.

She skittered to a stop, eyes going from the phone in my hand up to my face.

"This yours?" I asked, holding it out.

Silence.

Then a begrudging, "Yes."

I waved it lightly. "You going to take it?"

Her lips pressed flat, which I knew was a fucking shame because I'd kissed that luscious mouth and if it was pressed flat against anything, then it should be pressed flat to some part of my body.

And then I was thinking of all the parts she could press that mouth to.

And *then* my dick twitched.

Fuck.

She stepped forward and snatched the cell out of my hand.

And maybe the devil that had her biting me invaded *me* for a minute, because as she turned away, starting to stomp back into the front room, I couldn't help calling, "You're welcome."

She froze.

Spun slowly to face me.

Fuck, she was beautiful with her eyes blazing like that, the color high on her cheeks, her hair fanning out behind her. I'd be lying if I said I didn't notice that she was curved in all the right places, that my hands itched with the memory of briefly having those curves under my palms.

She strode toward me and jabbed a finger into my chest. "I don't know what your problem is," she hissed. "But—"

I captured that finger, brought it up to my mouth and nipped at the tip. "*You're* my problem, darlin'."

A shocked gasp paired with her trying to snatch her finger back. "You—y-you—"

"You're beautiful, darlin'," I whispered. "And I liked kissing you way too much. That's the honest truth," I added when it looked like she would argue. "But I'm not a good man and that— I shouldn't—" I shook my head, cutting off the words as familiar guilt came over me again. I hadn't been able to save Brooke's brother, hadn't bothered to look after Brooke. I hadn't even been able to fulfill my military contract because I'd been injured and—

Fuck. Enough.

But just like so often over the last year, I wasn't able to quiet the thoughts and insecurities.

Because at the end of the day, all I was good for was mixing a mean Cosmopolitan, pulling a beer with just the right amount of head from the tap, and running the occasional troublemaker from the bar.

Booze.

Bouncing.

Not infiltrating beautiful, innocent women's lives.

The anger faded from her face.

She went quiet for a long moment, that finger in my grip relaxing. But then she shocked the shit out of me by turning her hand and resting it along my jaw, cupping it gently. "You rescued my purse," she murmured. "You can't be that bad."

My breathing stalled at the gentle touch.

It was almost more intoxicating than the kiss. *Almost.*

"You don't know what I've done," I murmured, unable to believe the words were coming out of my mouth. "You don't know what I've seen. What—"

Sympathy in her blue-green eyes.

Then she rose on tiptoe, and her lips were on mine.

Heat.

Sweet as sugar.

Then the sugar disappeared.

"Dinner's at seven p.m.," she murmured, dropping back down to her feet. "72 Star Ridge. It's the yellow house on the corner with white trim."

She strode away, leaving me with my jaw dropped open, no doubt a shell-shocked expression on my face. But I managed to recover enough to ask her, just before she moved around the corner, "What's your name?"

Her feet stopped moving, those blue-green eyes drifted over her shoulder. "Iris."

I was still staring after her, thinking that was the absolute perfect name for her when I heard the front door open and shut.

The click of it closing made me jump.

Then realize I'd better figure out what I was going to bring to Iris's house for dinner.

Because I knew that I might be a lot of things—a failure, a shitty friend, a man who possessed an exceptionally powerful RBF—but my mom had at least raised me to be a good guest.

So, I didn't show up at someone's house emptyhanded.

And while I knew that I probably shouldn't be going down this minefield, that it was stupid to inflict myself on a woman I'd known two seconds after meeting her was way too good for me, I also wasn't going to miss out on a chance to show up at Iris's with flowers or a bottle of wine.

Because maybe I'd find exactly the right thing and she would smile at me like I'd hung the moon again, like she had when I'd pointed out her purse.

And maybe that meant she'd let me kiss her again.

FOUR

Iris

THE KNOCK at the door came precisely as the clock over my microwave turned from 6:59 P.M. to 7:00 P.M.

He was punctual.

He . . . was nameless.

My nerves threatened to swell up and overwhelm me for the hundredth time in the last twenty-four hours—well, the last eighteen hours because, yes, I'd been counting down the minutes, alternating between horror that I'd both kissed and invited a stranger to my house and excitement that I'd both kissed and invited a stranger to my house.

I didn't take risks.

Ever.

Well, that wasn't precisely true.

I hadn't taken risks up until the last month, until thirty-two days ago when I'd surprised Frank at our house for our anniversary, bringing dinner and booze and his favorite homemade cherry pie . . . and he'd clearly forgotten about the significance of the date.

Eleven years I had spent with him. From junior year of high school through college through starting a career. He'd given me a ring. We'd set a date.

And he was fucking a string of women on the side.

And he'd given me gonorrhea.

Fun times.

But I'd had the antibiotics, had been given the all clear, and I'd decided that I couldn't live in my small town in the foothills of the Sierra Nevadas any longer. I couldn't deal with the fact that *everyone* I knew and had grown up with, people who'd claimed they were my friends, people who'd interacted and talked with me on a regular basis, that not *one* of them had thought I should know that the man I was going to marry was sleeping with women who weren't me.

Well, that was probably because the women he was fucking were the same ones I'd once considered my friends.

Another knock had me blinking away the past and wiping my hands on a towel.

I hurried to the door, glancing through the window at the side and seeing that it was indeed the unnamed bartender from Bobby's.

He saw me through the glass, gaze drifting from my face to my toes then back up, and I watched as his eyes warmed, his expression relaxed, and he smiled. That smile had me freezing in place because it was huge and unapologetic . . . or maybe that wasn't quite the right word, because it was more like that grin lit up his face, removed any walls and barriers, and gave me a peek at something soft and vulnerable underneath.

And clearly, I was delusional if I thought I could read that much from a quirk of the lips.

Either way, I stood staring at him for far too long because he, still smiling, pointed to the door.

"Oh," I murmured, shaking my head slightly and reaching for the knob.

Doh. It would help to actually let the man whom I invited for dinner into my house. I flipped the lock and tugged open the door.

"Hi."

As far as greetings went, it wasn't the most original, but it tended to get the job done.

"Hi," he murmured.

Good. We were on the same level.

Inwardly snorting, I invited him in, taking the little potted Christmas tree he extended.

"I thought that since you'd just moved into the area, you might not have had time to decorate . . ." His words trailed off as he spun to take in my living room, which had been absolutely plastered with Christmas décor.

I like Christmas, okay?

Well, scratch that. I *love* Christmas, and when I'd moved out of the house Frank and I had bought—thankfully also the reason we'd put off our wedding for a year since our entire wedding fund had turned into house fund—I'd taken all of our Christmas stuff.

And because I loved the holiday, I had a lot.

Three artificial trees.

Twelve nutcrackers in various sizes.

Glittery wreaths and ribbons and festive tea towels. Pine-scented candles, strands of cranberries and popcorn, and—

Oh crap. It looked like my house had vomited up St. Nick. Which might be fine for someone I knew, someone who understood that my crazy extended to strictly this holiday and that I did not, in fact, have a shrine to all things Father Christmas in my bedroom.

But for this beautiful man, who was gorgeous enough to be gracing the silver screen, who was as sexy as a young Denzel Washington, and who definitely had that hint of his badassness from *The Equalizer*, me vomiting up St. Nick was less cool.

I bit my lip when he glanced back, eyes wide. "I don't think you need that—" he began and reached as though to take it back.

"No!" I said, clutching it to my chest. "No take-backs."

That smile again.

A curl of heat slid through my stomach, traipsing north and making my nipples bead against the cotton of my bra, but also maneuvering south, coiling between my thighs and dampening the material there.

"No take-backs?" he asked.

"Uh-uh," I muttered, still hugging the tree and neatly side-stepping him, just to make sure he didn't attempt to wrestle the tiny conifer from my grasp.

I had the perfect spot on my mantle, and I moved that way, shifting a couple of the nutcrackers to one side, straightening the festive fabric I'd draped there, and then settling the adorable little tree there.

Smiling, I touched one of the tiny gold globes that hung from a branch.

"I don't think I've heard anyone use the term *take-back* since high school," he said quietly, coming to my side, though his eyes were on my mantle. "Also, not sure if I should be worried by the sheer volume of nutcrackers you own, darlin'."

I turned to face him. "What's your name?"

Amusement in his deep brown eyes. "Brent."

"Brent what?"

"Collins." A beat. "And you're Iris what?"

"Hannigan."

Another smile. "So we've got Brent Collins and Iris

Hannigan in a house where Christmas exploded, and Iris possesses a shit-ton of nutcrackers that she can use to keep me in check if I get out of line."

I snorted. "They're purely for decorative purposes."

His eyes drifted down and back up. "That pretty little apron purely decorative, too?"

Him mentioning my apron had me gasping and sprinting for the kitchen as I remembered. "My pie!"

I loved baking and cooking and actually had a commercial kitchen just a couple of blocks away. It was part of the reason I'd moved into this neighborhood, part of the reason I'd put a full year's rent down on this cottage when I'd seen it. Even if the house hadn't been adorable and the commercial kitchen being rented from the same real estate company, being able to use my half of the proceeds from the sale of the house Frank and I had owned for something positive had been a major selling point. Being able to bake in a space that wasn't my own kitchen was another, especially when my contract with the local supermarkets for the last four years had recently expanded, as well as my online sales growing almost faster than I could keep up with.

What I *didn't* do was burn stuff.

Until today.

My face fell when I pulled out the cookie sheet with the tray of mini pies I'd baked.

Four because I loved pie.

Mini because I figured with only the two of us, we wouldn't be able to eat four entire pecan, cherry, pumpkin, and chocolate custard pies.

Four that had now become one.

Because only the chocolate was chilling in the fridge. The pecan, the cherry, and the pumpkin were . . . charcoal.

Not over-caramelized. Not golden brown on the edges.

Charcoal.

I stared at the once-pretty pies, the handcrafted crust, the lovely wreath decorations I'd cut out and strategically placed on the pumpkin, the Christmas tree on the pecan, the dancing gingerbread men on the cherry . . .

All charcoal.

Stupidly, my eyes stung.

It was only food, only dinner for a man I'd just met, only—

The cookie sheet and pot holder disappeared from my hand, was plunked onto the counter. Before I could protest to put it on a trivet, I found myself tugged toward the sink, and my fingers shoved under a stream of cool water.

I hadn't even realized they were stinging until the cold soothed the hurt.

But then the hurt was gone, and then the hurt ceased to exist. Because Brent was very close. His scent surrounded me, the masculine spice warming me from the inside out. I found myself taking a deep inhale, pulling the smell into my lungs, wanting to etch it on my soul so I could drop back into this moment any time I wanted.

Or perhaps, slightly less painfully, I could attempt to bottle it.

Both thoughts were impossible.

Both thoughts gave evidence for why I had lost my mind . . . and my filter.

"How in the world is it fair that you're so beautiful?" I blurted, staring up at the strong lines of his jaw and nose, the warm amber of his eyes. He was sporting a little stubble today, and I wanted to run my palm over it, feel the roughness catch my skin.

I was so caught up in the scent of him, in imagining my hands on his face and body, that it took my mind a moment to catch up with my words.

My eyes flicked to his face, saw his expression was unfathomable.

Probably looking for a quick exit. Frank had always tended to disappear when I went off on one of my tangents. And my tangents hadn't been anything like me wanting to etch some-one's scent on my soul or blurting out how beautiful someone was—though Brent was definitely in the gorgeous A-list celebrity bent. They'd been more along the lines of should I risk adding a dash of nutmeg to my apple pie recipe or is that too far out there?

Brent didn't reply.

Shit.

Strange woman inviting an almost-stranger home.

Now, I was rambling about his beauty.

Ugh. What was I going to do next? Offer to wear his skin like a suit?

I shuddered, the memory of the horror movies that Frank used to subject me to flaring through my brain. Too much. Too creepy. Too . . . much inner monologue when the near-stranger was staring at me, suddenly intent.

Because of the blurting, you moron!

So fucking stupid. My cheeks flared hot, my throat closed up, and I jerked my hand free of the water, quickly wiping it on my apron and turning for the counter where Brent had left the cookie sheet.

I picked up the discarded potholder and snagged the pies, dropping them one by one into the trash.

Pecan.

Shit-canned.

Pumpkin.

Peace out, mofo.

Cherry—

Brent snatched it and the potholder from my hands.

"What the fuck are you doing?"

I reached for it. "They're ruined."

"Because they're a little burned?" he asked, holding it aloft.

"A little?" I asked. "They're charcoal, totally inedible, and—"

He tugged off the burnt crust on the top, dumped it in the trash, then held it out. "Not charcoal, not inedible. See? Problem solved."

"I can't serve *that*."

He dipped a finger into the cherry pie, probably burning it worse than I'd burned mine, but then it was in his mouth, sucking off—

Sucking. Off.

Dear Lord.

I wanted to—

The sudden bolt of sexual desire that shot through me was so much stronger than anything I'd ever felt with Frank, what had driven me to invite him here, to participate in that kiss in his office, to be obsessed with his scent, his body. Then his finger slid out from between his lips with a soft *pop*, clean of filling, and I stared at his hand, at the finger, wondering about all of the things those body parts could do.

But this wasn't me.

I didn't obsess over men's bodies. I didn't want to jump them just because they smelled good.

I didn't kiss strangers.

I—

"This is delicious," he murmured. "We can scoop it out of the crust and eat the filling with ice cream."

"I—" A shake of my head. "But my crust. I—"

"That," he said, "I think you're right about." He broke off a blackened edge and popped it into his mouth, chewing then wincing. "Yup. Charcoal. But, darlin', just because something gets a little singed on the edges doesn't mean that it needs to be thrown away."

"It does when a girl makes her living baking pies just like these."

He set the pie on the counter, the potholder beneath it. "Are *you* the girl who makes her living baking pies?"

I wrinkled my nose then admitted, "Yes."

A shrug. "Well, I bet they're delicious." He dipped his finger into the pie again, and while unsanitary, I couldn't work up any real disgust or outrage. Not when he licked off the filling again, this time with a moan that made my pussy clench. "Yup. I could see it."

"Y-you can see it?"

He unleashed the smile. "Yup," he said again.

"Are you insane?"

Brent had been reaching for the pie again, finger extended, my thighs already trembling in anticipation of where that digit would end up, when I blurted the question. At my words, he froze, and one eyebrow went up.

"You're at my house on the invitation of a woman you don't know, an invitation I'm guessing you accepted because you're a nice guy who rescues purses and didn't want to make a lonely woman who's new in town feel bad for issuing you an inappropriate invite." I sucked in a breath. "And a lonely one who all but assaulted you in your office, just because there was mistletoe overhead, and I was desperate to kiss your gorgeous mouth.

"And then *you* show up with the most adorable little Christmas tree—which is amazing and cute and absolutely perfect, just like you—but then *I* burn dessert and it's my livelihood to *not* burn pies because I sold fifty thousand of them to grocery stores this year." I shoved my bangs out of my eyes. "And worse, now I've been going on and on about how beautiful you are and thinking about how much I want to kiss you again, when I definitely know I shouldn't be thinking any of those things because you're *way* out of my league."

I finally managed to shut my mouth, mainly because my embarrassment had reached a critical level and it stoppered up the words in the back of my throat.

Silence.

For a long, critically embarrassing, *horrifying* moment.

Finally, Brent took a step toward me. "You think I'm beautiful?"

I sighed, chin dropping forward to rest on my chest. "*That's* what you took from what I just said?"

He smiled. "You think I'm beautiful," he repeated, without the question mark this time, taking another step closer.

I groaned.

His fingers, one slightly sticky from the cherry pie, cupped my jaw. "You really sold fifty-thousand pies last year?"

I nibbled at the corner of my mouth. "Unburned ones. Yes."

He laughed and I swear, I felt that laughter enter my body, felt it fill my blood with champagne. *God*, he had an intoxicating laugh.

Sexy smile.

Hot as hell body.

That low, rasping chuckle that slid like honey down my spine.

"Sounds like I'm the one who's out of my league, darlin'," seeing as I'm a lowly bartender and you're the entrepreneur who's sold fifty-thousand pies."

I scoffed, waved a hand up and down my body. "Have you seen me?" I asked then pointed to him. "Have you seen *you?* Brent, you're solid muscle and have a movie star face. I'm a nerdy, overweight female who samples her pies far too often and has an obsession with Christmas. You shouldn't be here entertaining my invitation, not when you must have better things to do with your time, especially since—"

His mouth dropped to mine, lips slanting, tongue sliding home to tangle with mine, and in one heartbeat I went from thinking about all the reasons I was insane to have invited this man to my house when he should be spending the holiday with someone like Chrissy Teigen and not frumpy, flower-printed apron-wearing Iris Hannigan, to just . . . feeling.

Hot. Wet. Firm pressure. A coaxing tongue.

And desire. So much desire that it felt like lightning had struck in a drought-ridden forest, flames bursting to life, consuming the dry tinder in seconds.

My hands slid up his arms, wrapped around his biceps, clutching the granite-like muscles firmly as my body drifted forward, making contact with his, feeling his hard chest pressed against my soft breasts, getting so many different notes to the intoxicating scent of him—cinnamon and mint, sandalwood and . . . cherry.

I could smell the cherry on his mouth, could *taste* the cherry on his tongue.

He pulled back, still holding my jaw. "I didn't accept your invitation out of pity," he murmured. "I *saw* you at the bar, watched you out of the corner of my eye all night." My breathing stalled. He kept talking. "Looking beautiful. Looking so fucking lovely that I kept mixing up my orders. But I knew, just *knew* that you were the wrong kind of pretty, the kind of pretty that is too good for an asshole like me."

"Sounds like we both have confidence problems," I said.

Another blurt.

Fucking hell, I needed to find a way to control my tongue.

I ducked, more embarrassment making my cheeks hot, making my eyes slide down to the floor.

But then he laughed.

Warm, bubbling laughter that filled the room, that filled *me*.

What the hell was happening?

But then I didn't have time to process it because he stepped back, tugged at the tie of my apron and slipped it over my head. "You're right," he said, setting it on the counter. "Now darlin', what's for dinner?"

FIVE

Brent

IRIS SAT across from me at the table decorated with a trio of ceramic Christmas trees—the old-fashioned kind with the plastic lightbulbs that had to be pushed through the holes one-by-one—in the center of the dark oak. Silver garland interspersed with small glittery gold ornaments was woven in between them, drifting along the middle of the table to hang over either end.

But Iris amongst all the sparkle—the trees, the explosion of cheer shining in the room behind her—didn't fade into the background.

She was the brightest.

Or maybe that was just because I was entranced.

Absolutely, completely taken aback by this woman who'd nearly cried over burnt pies, who'd told me—and herself—that I lacked confidence, then had nearly blushed herself into a sunburn before nodding once after I'd agreed with her, turning away, then spinning back and shoving a stack of plates, napkins, and utensils into my hands, ordering me to, "Set the table."

Then she'd bustled around the kitchen, pulling out dishes and bringing them to the table, following that with serving spoons along with wine—for her—and beer—for me. And by the time she sat down, the flurry of movements encompassing the previous ten minutes, I'd almost needed to catch my breath.

Almost.

Because I wasn't quite certain that the reason I was out of breath wasn't because Iris looked absolutely radiant and adorable, especially with that streak of flour on her left cheek.

Dinner turned out to be a turkey casserole with mashed potatoes and dressing, grilled veggies, and sweet potatoes drizzled with honey, sprinkled with brown sugar, and crammed full of marshmallows.

She'd had me fix mine, added a dash of salt, then wrapped them both in foil and popped them into the oven, promising not to burn it.

She hadn't broken that promise.

And it was, hands down, the most delicious thing I'd eaten. Ever.

Until I'd tried her chocolate pie.

That quickly usurped the accessorized sweet potatoes and became the best thing I'd ever put in my mouth.

Ever.

Once everything had been settled onto the table, she had dished up my plate without preamble and then had begun quizzing me on my favorite television shows and movies.

I admitted a fondness for *The Office* and *Breaking Bad*. She named something called *Beauty and the Baker*. We both had loved every Marvel movie and were eagerly awaiting Black Widow's stand-alone film. Then we'd moved on to food—me, everything remotely edible because military base food really lowered culinary standards; her, everything under the sun that wasn't charcoal.

She'd blushed again at that, though her eyes had danced as she poked fun at herself.

And I'd had to force myself to keep my seat.

So fucking pretty.

I wanted to kiss her. I wanted to brush the flour off her cheek, wanted to kiss those plump rosebud lips.

Instead, I asked her about baking.

She told me about her commercial kitchen around the corner, how nice it was to be able to spread out and store her supplies, how it had been a relief to have a wall of ovens and a separate part of the space to box the pies, how she'd been able to hire a couple of high school kids to help her package, but that she'd let them have this week off so they could enjoy their time off from classes.

She sparkled. She charmed. She blushed and said, "Oh my God, I've been rambling about myself for too freaking long. Tell me, how long have you worked at Bobby's?"

And I knew then that even though I'd known this girl for all of a day, she was something special.

I told her I'd worked at Bobby's for about a year, that I'd been honorably discharged from the military, that I'd been at a loss of what I wanted to do with my life now that my parents were gone, and I'd needed a fresh start.

Kace had given me that fresh start.

My burly, tattooed bartender friend—and yes, I had tats, too, also yes, I enjoyed calling him my burly, tattooed bartender friend—because it drove him absolutely crazy, and driving Kace crazy filled my days with some of that Christmas sparkle that had exploded in Iris's house, except year-round. Still, we'd known each other for five years, both having served and our paths crossing at a wedding. When I'd been discharged a little over a year ago he'd offered me a gig. I'd taken it, and it worked. I was paying the bills while going back to school.

Because I was one of those cool thirty-three-year-olds whose days were filled with textbooks and college co-eds.

I'd told Iris that—well, not about the co-eds, but about going back to school as she'd served me up a slice of the most delicious chocolate pie I'd ever eaten. And I had a sweet tooth, so that was saying a lot.

"This is incredible," I said, scooping up a giant bite and shoving it into my mouth.

I shouldn't even be hungry, considering the amount of food I'd just consumed, the starch and carbs alone from the potatoes and stuffing should have sent my blood sugar skyrocketing before plummeting back down and sending me into a food coma. But when she also placed a bowl of cherry pie—sans crust, plus vanilla ice cream—in front of me, I didn't turn that down either.

I just gave her my thanks, finished up my chocolate pie, and started in on the cherry. "Thanks for inviting me," I said between bites. "This is way better than the frozen pizza I would have made myself."

She gasped. "Frozen?" A shudder. "Tell me you're not serious."

I lifted a brow. "I'm not serious?"

Her own fork, midway through her much smaller slice of chocolate pie, hit the table. "It's not hard to make your own dough. It's like three ingredients, and you let it rise and—"

"Will you show me?"

Lips opened then closed then opened again. "Um, what?"

"Will you show me how to make my own dough?" Three ingredients seemed doable, but mainly, this also seemed like a good way to ensure that I got to see her again.

Her brows drew down. "Tonight?"

I scooped up a spoonful of cherries and cream. "No. I think

I ate enough carbs that I'm almost at Defcon One of Pant-Splitting Stages."

"Oh." I liked to think that her expression held a twinge of disappointment. "Of course."

"How about tomorrow?"

Iris's gaze shot up. "Tomorrow?"

"Yeah," I said around bites. "The bar is closed tomorrow. I'm off school. I'd love to learn something new, especially if that something new involves pizza."

"Oh." Eyes back down, fork hovering over her pie.

"*Oh* what?" I asked, feeling some disappointment of my own. "Do you already have plans?"

She shook her head. "No, I just—" Another shake.

I reached across the table and covered her hand. "Just what?"

"I guess, I just thought I was blowing it, rattling on about baking, not tempering the Christmas crazy, almost crying about pies." She shrugged. "I figured you'd be beating a hasty retreat and—"

"Confidence."

Her expression turned confused. "What?"

"Remember that confidence thing we both need?" I asked, squeezing her fingers lightly. "Now seems like a good time for it."

She nibbled at the corner of her mouth. "You're right." A nod. "Tomorrow night. Pizza dough."

I lifted her hand, pressed a kiss to the back of her knuckles. "Cool, thanks, darlin'."

Uncertainty drifted across blue-green eyes. "That is—"

"Uh-uh," I said, flicking my tongue out. "No take-backs."

She froze, face incredulous, but then I started grinning, and she started grinning, and then we were both laughing.

When we'd finished, I nudged her bowl in her direction and said, "Now eat up, your pants need to feel as tight as mine."

More smiles. More laughter.

Then we settled in and finished our desserts.

Afterward, I forced her out of the kitchen to do the dishes, and later accepted a container of leftovers—because they were delicious and I'd work out extra hard if it meant I could keep eating them.

And when I left that night, I stole a kiss.

Because, look at that, she had mistletoe hanging over the front door, and I couldn't let that go to waste.

Yeah. That Christmas explosion she'd made happen definitely had its perks.

SIX

Iris

"THAT'S IT," I told Brent the next night. "Now, we just wait for it to double in size, roll it out, put the toppings on, and then bake it. Ten to fifteen minutes after that, we'll have the best pizza you've ever tasted."

I didn't tell him that it was actually one of my traditions to make a turkey, cranberry sauce, and stuffing laden pie, combining all the best leftovers with even more carbs, nor did I tell him that no one had ever cared enough about what I cooked to ever want to learn part or all of the process. Not my friends, not my parents, not Frank.

It was probably a little sad that I was just now realizing how messed up that was.

Not that I'd expected them to hop in the kitchen with me. Or to push up their sleeves and join in when I'd been in the weeds, overwhelmed with orders and hopelessly behind—not every time anyway.

Occasionally would have been nice.

Even just offering to help would have been fine.

But they hadn't and . . . I hadn't thought to ask.

I'd put my head down, built up resentment that they hadn't, and I'd gotten really good at thinking that all the problems in my life were because of everyone else.

That I hadn't played any role in them.

I was realizing now that I'd done my part.

Ugh.

I didn't want to think deep thoughts, to reevaluate my inner self. I wanted to enjoy my time with the beautiful man in my kitchen because who knew how long his interest would last.

There. Done. Moving on.

Except, when I glanced up, realizing that I'd been lost in my head for far too long for polite conversation, Brent was staring down at me, expression soft.

I sighed, dropped my eyes to the bowl in front of me, fussing with the plastic wrap, making sure it was secure so a skin wouldn't form on the dough. He waited while I stashed the bowl in the oven that was set to "Proof" then took my hand and led me to the family room.

Christmas extravaganza was in a slightly diminished form. I began packing up items one box at a time after the holiday. This reduced the Christmas craze, but also extended it, because I ended up being able to keep my holly, jolly happy with me for a little bit longer.

Die Hard—the first and best, and also the best holiday movie of them all—was cued up to stream. The plan was for Brent and me to binge on caramel and regular popcorn, to thoroughly ruin our dinner, and then to make the pizzas and get even more stuffed.

I'd spent the day looking forward to seeing him, counting the minutes down in a way that should have been scary but was somehow not.

Because it was easy.

Because I could talk to him, could say whatever thought crossed through my mind, and I knew he'd just roll with it.

And I'd showed plenty of crazy.

Not, least of which, was this moment.

"You ponder it out?" he asked gently.

"I don't know if I pondered it all out," I admitted. "But I did realize, unfortunately, that I played a role in everything that happened."

Picking up the remote, I went to start the movie, but he snagged it from my fingers and set it next to his thigh. "Nope." A shake of his head. "What put that sad look in your eyes, darlin'?"

"It's nothing," I muttered, reaching for the controller. "And way too heavy for a chill hangout night."

"Iris."

"Plus, we don't know each other. I've already given you way too many blurts for the forty-eight hours of our acquaintance. In fact, I think I'm at my blurt limit." I lunged for the remote, but he caught my hands against his chest. "You definitely don't need to know that my high school boyfriend, who was also my college boyfriend, and then my after-college fiancé was screwing around on me. Or that the girls he was sleeping with were my friends. Or that I just realized that not one of those friends or Frank had ever shown any interest in learning a recipe or helping out when I was swamped with orders. Or—"

I clamped my lips shut, ending the blurt of all blurts. The blurt that decimated every single blurt limit.

Fucking. Hell.

I dropped my gaze, not able to hold the warm amber of Brent's eyes, not wanting to see the realization in them of my crazy . . . or worse, pity. He wore a fitted blue T-shirt, and it popped against the russet of his skin, highlighted the tattoos inked into his arm.

Tattoos I wanted to know the meaning of.

Tattoos I wanted to trace with my tongue.

Tattoos—

He wasn't saying anything.

Like he had clammed up, a heavy and oppressive silence filling the space between us.

Double. Fucking. Hell.

But . . . he also didn't let me go. His hands covered mine on his chest, hot and a little rough. Callouses from someone who was active, who did honest work. Callouses similar to mine from all the whisking and stirring I did on a daily basis. Callouses—

Shit. More silence. Even heavier, although I felt a trace of impatience along with it.

His words, when he finally spoke, told me why. "Look at me, darlin'." Not gentle or soft, but a command. I followed it, forcing my stare from the stitching on the collar of his shirt up to his eyes. "Your fiancé?"

I nibbled at the corner of my mouth. "I shouldn't have said all that."

"Iris." His eyes narrowed, that amber heating, but not in a good way or a sexy way—okay, it *was* both—but the point was, his eyes weren't increasing in temperature because he was turned on. They were sparking with frustration.

I didn't want him frustrated with me.

I also didn't want to lie to myself any longer.

And . . . why the fuck shouldn't I tell the truth? Yes, I was beginning to take responsibility for the fact that I wasn't perfect in my relationship, but Frank had cheated. Repeatedly. And my friends had been complicit in that behavior. Further that, if he'd had a problem, he should have come to me and addressed the problem.

It would have hurt for him to break up with me.

But it had hurt a lot more to have the breadth of his deception crash into me like a tsunami taking out houses on the coast —knocking into them, crushing them to pieces, washing them inland before stealing them out to sea.

It had caused so much damage.

And for what?

Brent placed one hand on the back of my neck. "It seems like some pieces are coming together in your mind, darlin', so I'll just say this." He paused, waited for my eyes to come back to his. The intensity still there, the anger gone. Because this time, it was tempered with respect. "Frank was a fucking idiot to have let you go."

"I'm not perfect," I said, slipping my hands free of his still resting against his chest. I slid one to his shoulder, leaned in. "But I'm starting to see that you're right. Frank *was* a fucking idiot."

Brent unleashed his smile.

My panties got wet.

I leaned in, hesitated.

"You gonna kiss me?" he murmured. "Or do I have to go and find some mistletoe?"

I closed the distance between us, and on the day after Christmas, *Die Hard* paused on TV, my body draped over the lap of a gorgeous, kind man who called me *darlin'* and kissed me like I was the most precious woman in the universe, I thought that perhaps meeting Brent had changed everything.

Because it felt like my life would never be the same.

Then his tongue slipped between my lips, his hands shifted, and he pulled me more snugly against his hips, and I lost track of time.

So much so that I forgot all about the pizza dough in the oven.

———

AN HOUR LATER, I stared into the oven, to the bowl overflowing with the severely over-proofed pizza dough, and groaned.

"It's ruined."

Brent was leaning a hip against the counter, arms crossed, face nonplussed. "Is this one of those cherry pie ruined scenarios, or is it *really* ruined?"

Sighing, I grabbed the bowl and dumped its contents into the trash. "Ruined *ruined*," I muttered, glaring at him. "You're not allowed to come within a hundred yards of my commercial kitchen. You're too distracting."

He just grinned.

I pulled out my phone, opened DoorDash. "Your choice. My treat."

He pulled out *his* cell. "How about *your* choice, and it's my treat."

I sighed. "Brent."

He smiled wider. "Iris."

"I ruined dinner," I said, plunking my hands onto my hips. "I should pay."

A step closer, his scent drifting over me. "*We* ruined dinner," he said, fingers drifting up my arm, slipping behind my neck, and weaving into my hair. "But you bought supplies for both, so I'm paying."

"Frank never argued with me about paying."

"I think it's already been established that Frank is an asshole," he said. "I'm not trying to be all steroidal alpha-male, but if a girl I'm interested in tries to pay, I'm not letting her."

I leaned back, glared up at him. "*Letting?*"

He shrugged then repeated, "Letting."

My temper flared, my lips parted to fire off a retort . . . and then I saw the twinkle in his eyes.

He was messing with me.

The twerp.

"You're annoying," I said, even though I was smothering my own smile.

"That's true," he agreed. "Kace says it on the regular." A beat before he held up his cell. "So, letting me pay?"

"Me letting *you*," I replied, not bothering to fight my smile any longer. "Yup, that's right."

He snorted but didn't otherwise reply. Instead, he stayed close as he scrolled through the restaurants on the screen. "Still in the mood for pizza?"

My stomach rumbled in affirmation.

A flash of white. "Pizza it is. Do you like Indian food? There's this fusion place not too far away, and their tandoori pie is beyond delicious."

As a matter of fact, I loved Indian food. "Is it spicy?"

"Is it Indian food?" he countered.

"True." I giggled. "Well, the good news is I do like spicy things."

He waggled his brows. "I'm hoping you're saying that in reference to my spicy personality."

I snorted. "I'm starting to understand why Kace says you're annoying."

"It's a skill I've honed over many years." He pressed the screen a few more times. "Okay, so pizza is an hour out"—he pocketed his cell then took my hand, started drawing me back to the couch in the other room—"so we've got time to see John McClane blow some shit up."

"And eat caramel corn," I said, letting myself get drawn along, partly because he was strong and fighting him would take effort I was feeling too lazy to exert after having spent the last hour in his arms, enjoying his mouth on mine, his hands on my body. But although I'd thoroughly enjoyed those kisses, I mostly let him lead me to the other room because I liked spending time with him. He was funny and kind, and had a no-nonsense way about him that I really appreciated after Frank's duplicity. I liked how carefully he held me against him, as though I were important, but not like I was fragile.

And I liked how he teased me.

Gently, not in a mean way, and paired with a self-deprecating smile as he equally poked fun at himself.

I liked the smiles.

I liked the laughter.

Both made me feel lighter than I had in years, and the pain from Frank, the hole I'd opened, and the uncertainty I felt in leaving home and everyone I knew, shrank.

How two days could change a person's life so unequivocally, I couldn't quite believe, but it *had* changed. And not just because of Brent and how he made me feel, but also because the distance away from home, from what I was realizing was a black hole, emotional-vampire-filled drama den, had given me clarity.

I could do this.

I didn't need my parents. I didn't need my so-called friends. I didn't need Frank.

And perhaps understanding that meant I would be able to let in more people like Brent.

"You're pretty when you're pondering," Brent said.

I came out of my head enough to realize that he'd led me to the couch, had tucked me into his side. "I'm sorry," I murmured. "I'm not used to having my head in the clouds this often. Usually, I'm a feet-on-the-ground, eyes-forward, plowing-on kind of person." I wrinkled my nose. "Which is probably why I missed the fact that my fiancé was sleeping with every available female in the vicinity."

"Men who are going to cheat, cheat," he said. "Nothing you did or didn't do would have changed that. But a real man would have talked through his problems with you about your relationship rather than do that sneaking around bullshit."

My nose stayed wrinkled. "It's not fair that you're funny, kind, gorgeous, *and* smart."

He grinned. "I'm not sure about any of that, but I'll take the compliment."

I dropped the fake consternation and touched his jaw. "Good. I mean it. And . . . thanks for taking a leap in coming over yesterday, then weeding through the Christmas crazy and the pie meltdown to hang out. It's nice to make a new friend."

"Why is that phrased like a kiss-off when we have two large pizzas coming?"

My jaw fell open. "Two *large* pizzas? How are we going to eat that much?"

"I think you forget that I saw you go to town on carbs last night. It's not a matter of how we're going to eat the two large pies, but whether two large pies is enough to fill that hollow leg"—he patted my thigh, and yes, my pussy flared to attention at having his hand so close to that particular body part—"of yours."

I was concentrating so fiercely on the space between my thighs that it took me a moment to process what he'd said.

Brent laughed at my glare and kissed the top of my nose. "Also, just to be clear, I'm not here to make a friend." A heavy moment as he held my gaze, waited for his words to sink in. And they did, though they were paired with no small amount of disbelief. "I like you, darlin'. More than any woman I've met in the last few years, and more than anyone I've met maybe ever. *You're* smart and beautiful and funny, and it's no trial to walk a few blocks to hang out with you." Another light brush of his mouth, this time on my forehead. "Even if you do have an insane number of nutcrackers collecting dust on that mantle."

"Collecting dust?" I gasped. "I just wiped everything—"

He kissed me, thoroughly, intently, long enough to have my lungs burning from a lack of oxygen. Then he released me and cuddled me into his side. "Two pizzas. That's enough." He picked up the remote, pressed play. "Especially because I know you made a fresh pumpkin pie."

I had, so I didn't argue.

I'd also whipped up some fresh cream, adding a dash of cinnamon, because I was going wild and really living my best life now. But I didn't tell Brent that. Instead, I cuddled closer, leaned my head on his shoulder, happy that he didn't want a friend.

Because I didn't want one either.

Or *only* one, anyway.

Then I kept my eyes glued on the screen and watched as John McClane's tank top got progressively more stained.

The doorbell rang when duct tape joined the party.

Brent paused the movie, told me to stay put, then crossed to the front door to retrieve the pizzas.

I didn't stay put.

I got plates and napkins, a refill of my wine, a fresh beer for him, and I returned to the family room just as he reached the table. Instead of getting huffy that I ignored him, like Frank would have done—well, it would have been *me* getting the plates and drinks, *me* going to the door and retrieving the pizzas because his ass would have stayed on the couch—but instead of being upset that I'd gotten up, he took the drinks from my hand then the plates and napkins, before brushing a kiss over my lips and nudging my butt onto the cushions.

Then he loaded a plate with two slices of pizza—one tandoori, one that was covered in a variety of vegetables and looked delicious—and handed it to me.

He was next to me on the couch a minute later, his own plate of pizza balanced on his lap, and when I reached for my wine, even though the movie was at its crescendo, he grabbed it and handed it to me.

It was strange and wonderful and . . . the teeniest bit unnerving, how in tune we seemed to be.

Because I knew when he wanted another slice, when he was reaching for *his* drink, and I didn't think twice about handing it to him either, nor about the kiss I brushed on his cheek when he took my empty plate and set it on the table when he'd finished.

In sync.

I didn't think I'd ever been so in sync with someone in my life.

And probably that should have taken unnerving and ramped it to freaked-the-fuck-out, but instead, it took unnerved and made it disappear, instead it allowed me to keep drinking my wine as *Die Hard* turned to *Die Hard 2,* then appreciate that he paused the sequel and did the dishes while I plated dessert.

Then it made me fall a little in love, when I woke up the next morning, tucked safely in bed, the blankets pulled up to my chin, and a note on the nightstand from Brent.

> *Hope you had sweet dreams, darlin'.*
> *-B*
> *P.S. I promise to keep two hundred yards from your*
> *kitchen, if you promise to come into the bar tonight. My*
> *shift starts at 7.*

I got up, showered, and headed to my kitchen, fulfilling orders and packaging on my own, relieved that my staff would be back the following day.

But since I did have the space to myself, I took the opportunity to whip up something that wasn't expressly available on my order form or online store, and I made sure to set a timer.

This time the pizza dough was absolutely perfectly risen.

And I didn't think Brent would mind having pizza for dinner two nights in a row, because I knew my leftover-turkey-cranberry-stuffing-covered pie was the best one I'd ever made.

Definitely not charcoal.

SEVEN

Brent

YEAH, I could dig my girl walking into Bobby's, smiling up at me like that every single day.

Especially when she carried a box, holding it up with a cat-ate-the-canary smile that made me want to kiss her right in front of everyone.

And I meant *everyone*.

The bar was packed. Brooke was in her corner, typing away in her own fictional world, various groups of regulars dotted around the space, taking up their typical tables and booths, but the rest of the customers *weren't* regulars. Which was good for the bar's and Kace's, part-owner of the place, bottom line. But it wasn't great for me having time to eat whatever deliciousness was percolating out of the box Iris had brought in nor finding the opportunity to kiss her luscious mouth, to taste her smirk on my tongue.

I nodded toward end of the bar where Brooke was sitting, waiting until I saw her moving before I pulled out the stool I'd stashed behind the bar earlier, having purposely ignored Kace's confused look.

I stuck it next to Brook's stool.

"Brooke, meet Iris," I said to my former best friend's little sis when Iris came close. I knew she would be nice to Iris and knew they could both use more friends in their lives, especially ones who would look out for each other rather than be catty-back-stabbers.

"Iris," I said, brushing my knuckles over her cheek. "This is Brooke. She puts up with my grumpy ass . . ." I paused, smirked over at Kace, who'd come up. "*friend*, Kace."

Kace narrowed his eyes.

"Kace, this is Iris. Iris, Kace. My grumpy, burly, tattooed boss."

Kace rolled his eyes but extended a hand to Iris, who shifted her box to the side so she could shake it. "Nice to meet you," he said. "What can I get you to drink?"

"I got it," I said.

Her gaze met mine.

"House merlot, right?"

She nodded. "Thanks."

I turned away, reaching for a glass, even though I was seriously encroaching on Kace's station, but she stopped me with a hand on my wrist.

"Pizza," she murmured, lifting the box, "that comes with perfectly risen dough."

"Thanks, darlin'," I said, flipping my palm over to capture her fingers in mine, squeezed lightly. "I'll have to save it to eat during my dinner break, but it smells incredible." I snagged the box. "Let me put this somewhere safe, grab your wine, get ahead on orders, then I'll come back and chat."

"Go," she ordered then smiled. "Also, while it's better hot, it's almost as good cold." Shifting, she parked herself on the stool

I'd brought out, then pulled out a book from her purse. "And don't worry about me. I've come prepared to entertain myself."

I nodded, started to turn away.

Then turned back, mouth dropping open.

Then looked at Brooke, caught her gaze, and let my eyes drop back to the cover. She frowned, but then let her own gaze drift down to the book, eyes crinkling with mischief as a smile spread over her face. "What do you think of it?" she asked Iris.

I opened my mouth, but Iris cut me off before I had the chance to intervene. "Oh my God, it's amazing! Have you read Brooke McAlister before? She's on my instant buy list. I love her books so much!"

I didn't think Brooke had thought through the actual conversation before she'd started down this path.

One, because my Brooke—well, *Kace's* Brooke—*was* Brooke McAlister.

And two, because my-slash-Kace's Brooke was also terrible at taking compliments.

I grinned. "Funny story," I said, certain there was now mischief in *my* eyes, "is that *this* Brooke"—I indicated Brooke, whose cheeks were now flaring bright red—"is—"

"Brent," Brooke warned.

I ignored her. "*That* Brooke." I tapped the book's cover.

Iris's mouth dropped open. "No way."

"Yes, way." Brooke smiled shyly. "Thanks for reading them."

"Omg, reading is the least of what I do to them—" Iris broke off, shook her head. "Sorry, that sounded really freaking weird. But my point was that, yes, I read them. Also, yes, I devour them. I preorder the eBooks so they can hit my Kindle at nine p.m. the night before release day, then stay up all night reading, then I order the paperback to be delivered on release day so that I can reread the story on *actual* book pages." She sighed, held the novel to her chest. "You write the best male characters. I swear Jace was my favorite."

Kace chose that moment to pop his head in, muttering. "Don't want to cock-block, bro, but I really need a hand."

I nodded. "Sorry. I'll—"

"Wait," Iris said, and I stopped, not realizing that she wasn't looking at me in the least. Her gaze was flicking between Kace and Brooke, and a wide grin had broken out on her face. "*You're* Jace?" Her lips parted on a slow exhale. "Whoa. That's—"

"Fiction," I growled, shoving between them and now seriously regretting having put my woman on Kace's end of the bar.

What had I been thinking?

Kace was . . . a fucking model. Every woman drooled after him, wanted to get in his pants. Iris would be—

"Did you really steal Brooke's credit card?"

Kace's brows pulled down.

"That means yes," Brooke whispered, lips curved at the corner. "And while my Kace was the initial inspiration for the book's hero, I did make Jace much more alpha, much more of an asshole, and much more stubborn."

"Hey," Kace protested. "I'm alpha."

"He's not," Brooke stage whispered. "I love the man, but what I love the most is that even though he strives to take care of me, even though he can be pushy and demanding sometimes, that he is *not* an alpha. He's a beta or even what I'd consider a pussy cat."

Kace made a strangled noise.

I was suddenly feeling a lot better, especially when Iris nodded and said, "Alphas. Fun to read. Not so fun to live with."

"I'd take Kace over Jace, every day of the week," Brooke said. "He's a much better kisser than a fictional hero and that goes doubly so for in the—"

Now it was my turn to make a strangled noise.

Kace glanced over at me, made a sympathetic face. "We've gotta get out of here, dude, before we hear more shit we shouldn't."

"Gems of the female psyche you mean," Brooke teased. "But seriously, that guy needs a beer before he loses his shit." She pointed to a man who was angrily occupying a stool on my end of the bar. "Clean up your stations, take care of your customers, and let Iris and me chat."

I glanced at Iris, and her eyes came to mine, still wide but filled with excitement.

So, I nodded, took off for my end, stowed the box carefully because I sure as shit wasn't sharing my food spoils with Jace-slash-Kace burly, broody, bartender beauty extraordinaire. Then I washed my hands and started running through orders.

I'd been working—taking requests, pulling beers, mixing drinks, pocketing tips—for almost fifteen minutes before I managed to take a breath.

Kace glanced up from the tray he was filling for one of the waitresses, a plethora of cocktails for one group of their regulars —including Heather O'Keith, who owned a small portion of Bobby's still, but had sold the rest of her portion of the business to Kace. He signaled to the waitress that the drinks were ready to go and then crossed over to me.

"Um, it's been three days since I've seen you, bro," he said. "Want to clue me in to what happened?"

My eyes flicked toward Iris, not that they'd been doing much else aside from the bare minimum required for me to focus on pouring the drinks but not overfilling them. She was still chatting away with Brooke, her color high, her expression excited. Brooke, for her part, used to be exceptionally shy but had come out of her shell in the last year. Plus, I'd had the feeling that she and Iris would hit it off.

Just so long as she didn't hit it off with *Kace*.

Asshole.

I grunted, turned away to pull a few more beers and set them on the server's tray.

Kace was standing there, looking perfectly at ease, except for one raised brow.

"She came into the bar on Christmas Eve. I noticed her, she left. Came back because she left her purse."

"And now you're saving seats and plunking her ass next to Brooke's?"

"She's too good for me."

"Know that feeling well, bro," he said. "So, you gonna stay away from this too-good girl?"

I shrugged. "I probably should."

"That's not a no."

It wasn't. Because I knew that I wasn't a great guy, even though I had a checkered past, the least of which was not being there for the sister of my best friend when that best friend had lost his life; the most of which was the fact that I hadn't been able to save that best friend in the first place. But I knew that even despite those things, I still wanted Iris.

Hayden had a person to go back to.

I'd had no one.

He'd died. I'd lived.

It should have been the other way around. But I still wanted Iris.

"You deserve to be happy."

I shrugged. Maybe logically, I knew that. Maybe logically, I *wanted* that. But also mixed in with that logic was the fact that I knew if Hayden hadn't thrown himself in front of that fucking IED then I would have died, and he would have lived.

Maybe he would have had the bum back I'd spent a long fucking time in physical therapy working through, but he would have still been alive. He wouldn't have had the trauma from nearly dying of his injuries, wouldn't have had the flashbacks and PTSD or the brain injury that had eventually driven him to take his own life.

And even having all of that running through my brain, knowing that the better man didn't live, I also knew that I wasn't going to be able to walk away from Iris. She was . . . special. Which, I got, sounded cliché and sappy and so damned stupid for just knowing her for three days.

But I'd seen the Christmas explosion.

I'd seen the passion for her career.

I'd felt the way she'd curled into me, smelled the scent of her shampoo when she fell asleep on my chest, had my heart squeeze and expand and constrict with hope and fear when she trusted me enough to fall asleep.

Because she felt it, too.

One conversation, one kiss, and there seemed to be an invisible connection between the two of us.

I glanced up and watched her again, smiling at her gestures, wanting to know what she was saying to Brooke, even though it was probably more of her mooning over the fictional Kace-based hero, and so I probably didn't *want* to know after all.

As though she felt me staring, her eyes came up and she smiled.

At me.

Broken me. Unworthy me.

And I knew that even though I wasn't nearly what she deserved, I also didn't possess the strength to let her go.

I WORKED THE NEXT NIGHT. Iris came in to say a quick, "Hi," and brought dinner, which we ate together at her stool, her sitting atop it, me crowding into her, taking the chance to be close, to smell her, to soak up her smiles.

But all too soon we finished eating and she had to head home, since she had an early morning at her kitchen the next day.

I nodded at Kace, told him I'd be back in fifteen, and because everything was quiet, took the opportunity to walk Iris home.

"What are you baking tomorrow?" I asked, lacing our fingers together, stomach pleasantly full of the chicken pot pie she'd brought me for dinner.

It was a hell of a lot better than the wings and fries I normally inhaled while on shift, mainly because I wasn't choking down raw celery in an attempt to be healthy.

Buttery crust, well-cooked veg, juicy and tender chicken.

Yeah, it wasn't hard eating Iris's food.

She leaned her head on my arm as we walked, and I realized her pause in answering came from her doing some mental math. "Two hundred and thirty-seven pies. All mini-sized—eighty apple with my special, secret recipe sugar-dusted lattice tops, one-hundred chocolate custard, all decorated with silver and gold for a corporate New Year's party, along with an additional fifty mini-cheesecakes topped with mixed berry compote for the non-chocolate lovers, three pumpkin, three cherry, and one pecan." A beat. "Not going to ask?"

I glanced down at her, smiling. "I was checking your math."

"Hmph," she said, then lifted her head from my shoulder so she could reach into her purse and pull out her keys. "The last seven are for you." A shrug. "Well, for you, Kace, and Brooke."

My eyes narrowed at the thought of Kace getting her pies.

And yes, I knew I was feeling possessive, knew it was ridiculous, but she already had the fictional Kace to drool over. Why did the asshole need her pies, too? Brooke, I got. She was sweet, deserved something sweet in return.

Iris smacked me lightly. "So scowly," she murmured, rising on tiptoe to slant her lips across mine. "Because I mentioned Kace?"

I growled. "Don't say his name."

She grinned. "He's in a committed relationship."

I grunted.

"And madly in love with Brooke."

Another grunt.

"Brooke, who promised me an advanced copy of her book if I traded her a pie."

More grunting.

"Who also said that she wouldn't share said pie with Kace."

That made me smile.

Iris laughed. "God, Brent, I'm so happy I met you."

I touched her cheek. "You can't know how lucky I am that you left your purse behind." She sucked in her breath and I bent my head, taking her lips and kissing her like I'd been desperate to do from the first moment she'd shown up in Bobby's the previous week. Just a few nights and my soul had been indelibly marked.

That should have been terrifying.

And yet, I wasn't feeling the least bit scared, especially when she leaned in and whispered in my ear, "FYI, you get the most pies, because you're the best," and then nipped my earlobe.

Goose bumps lifting on my skin.

My cock going hard.

But it wasn't until she said, "They're for you. And they'll be the best ones, I promise," that I felt my heart roll over in my chest.

"Darlin'," I said roughly, wrapping my arms around her and tugging her close, knowing that even though only a few days had passed between us, even though I was definitely scowly, even though I was feeling possessive and didn't want to share *any* part of her with the rest of the world, that I was all in.

But she wasn't mine yet.

I *wanted* her to be mine, wanted her to have me in return, even if it was stupid, even if the trade wasn't remotely fair . . . I wanted her in my life.

If my mom was still alive, she'd have told me off for jumping into something so quickly.

If my dad was still alive, he would have told me that my jumping into something with a good woman like my mom had been, like Iris was, would be the smartest thing I'd ever done.

Impossible to please them both, even if we were on opposite sides of the grave.

But I still knew which one was going to be smiling down at me, telling me I'd made the smart choice.

And that parent would be my dad.

Then begrudgingly, my mom.

Because . . . Iris and her pies. Iris and her sweet smile. Iris and her passion for Christmas, the hurt in her eyes when she told me of the betrayal of her ex, her friends.

Because Iris was special and deserved to be with someone who recognized exactly how wonderful that special was.

Which probably didn't make sense.

Or maybe it was all the big feelings filling me to bursting that had my mind going in ever-increasing circles. Those circles moving in one direction, growing larger and larger to encompass everything wonderful about the woman in front of me—the need to watch out for her, to care for her as she deserved, to prove I was worthy to make myself at home inside her soul, to promise that I'd make a safe space inside my soul for her in return, that had me doing some blurting of my own. "Do you want to go on a date with me?"

She frowned, head tilting to the side. "I thought . . . I kind of thought that's what we were already doing?"

It wasn't no.

It also wasn't yes.

"I want to take you out to a nice restaurant. To dress up and hold your hand over dinner, to tempt you into dessert, then to drive you home and kiss you on this doorstep," I said, cupping both of her cheeks. "I want you to have a nice night, to do this right. Because I'm into you, darlin', and I don't think I want to let you go."

Her breath caught on an audible inhale.

Then, "I'm into you, too."

My pulse had been thundering in my veins, but her words calmed the pounding, settled my heart.

At least until she said, "But—"

Thundering again, pounding so loud against my eardrums that I could barely hear her, and I definitely missed the mischief in her blue-green eyes. *That* I didn't deduce until after the next exchange.

"You have two things wrong."

I swallowed hard.

"First, you never have to tempt me into dessert."

I relaxed, caught the mischief and smiled. "And the second?"

"I don't think I want you to stop with just kissing me on this doorstep," she murmured, body drifting forward, brushing against mine and making dread slide through me. "I'd be inviting you in, inviting you upstairs."

Fuck. I hadn't gotten that far.

I *should* have gotten that far.

I *should* have known it would lead there.

But I just . . . hadn't let my mind *go* there.

Because I had a secret. A big, fucking secret that I needed to clue Iris into, one that would likely have all of her *I'm into you, too* turning into pity then turning into *Yeah, no. That won't work for me.*

I had to tell her.

Now. Give her the out. Give myself the break of saving my heart from further damage when she invariably left.

A gentle palm stroked along my jaw. "Brent, are you okay?"

"Iris—"

My cell rang.

She stepped back. "It's probably Kace," she said. "You should answer it."

I reached into my back pocket and silenced it. "No. It's not important. Iris—"

It immediately began ringing again.

"Answer it, honey," she said, pulling my cell from my pocket and handing it to me.

Kace's name flashed on the screen. *Shit.* I'd been gone too long.

"It's a yes," she said, swiping a finger on the screen before putting it up to my ear. "To the date." Then she waved, opened the front door, and disappeared inside.

I opened my mouth to tell her to wait, to stop, but then Kace's voice drifted through the speakers.

"I'm sorry, man, but there's been a disturbance in the bar."

Fuck.

"I need you back here now."

I didn't follow Iris inside, didn't tell her the secret that was weighing on me. I turned in the direction of Bobby's and hauled my ass back.

Later, I wished I'd stayed, had told her the truth right then and there.

But by that time, it was too late.

EIGHT

Iris

I WAS GETTING ready for a date.

My first real date, if I was being honest with myself.

Because I was just discounting everything from the Frank Period in my life. A.D. and B.C., except I was going to more aptly call them, B.F. and A.F.—as in, Before Frank and After Frank.

Yeah. That.

And after was going to be so much better than *during*.

I slipped into my killer suede booties, arranged the cowl neck of my burgundy sweater dress to show just a little more cleavage.

Because why not?

I'd spent too much time in my life worrying about how things could go wrong, fluttering around, working my ass off to prevent them from happening, and . . . I was done, dammit.

I'd done everything possible to make things work with Frank, including making myself feel small, putting what I wanted on the back burner.

I'd wanted to rent a kitchen sooner, but he'd convinced me that I was going to fail, that it would be a risky financial decision to rent something. But then he'd used the money for a second Master's degree, and while I appreciated him wanting to learn, had wanted to do my part to help build our future, to facilitate his dreams, I also knew now that I deserved to have some of my dreams come true, too.

And I was starting by going on a date with a funny, kind, gorgeous man and continuing by not questioning everything that didn't seem to make sense between us—including but not limited to: he was beautiful, I was not; he was a ten, I was a six on a good day; he was hilarious, I could occasionally make someone chuckle—

"Enough, Iris," I muttered.

No more denigrating when I should be lifting myself up . . . because just . . . enough.

It was funny—not *ha-ha funny* but *strange funny*—how I could proceed along a path without deviating, without seeing how fucked up it was for years, but that one conversation with Brooke had tipped me over the edge.

I'd been thinking a lot since I found out about Frank.

But I'd still been shouldering more than my fair share of the burden.

Then, two nights before, Brooke—and squee! I was somehow on a first name basis with Brooke *Freaking* McAlister, my favorite author—but what she'd said hadn't necessarily been book-related. She'd been talking about Kace, about taking a leap with him and finding the courage to put her heart on the line.

"I realized I could either continue to live on the periphery," she'd said, tucking a strand of her long, red hair behind one ear. "*Or* I could just live."

I'd smiled, teased her, even though those words collided heavily with my soul. "You should write books or something."

Brooke had grinned. "I've definitely got the *or something* part down," she'd said. "At least, according to some of my readers," she'd added when I'd given her a questioning look. "Oh, it's nothing. I just got a lovely email this morning accusing me of writing filth, and the lady told me if she owned a car, she would use it to run over her Kindle, in hopes of it erasing the 'disgusting tripe' that had crossed its screen."

Perspective.

The living or being on the periphery part from Brooke.

But also, the perspective that someone could think that the stories I so enjoyed, the slice of escapism and fun and, yes, occasionally the very steamy sex scene, were disgusting and horrible and something to be scrubbed out of existence.

I didn't want to be scrubbed out of existence. Or live constantly on the sidelines.

"That would turn out to be a very expensive eBook," I'd told Brooke. But inside I'd felt my realization like a punch to the gut. For so long, I'd seen myself in one way, seen my life moving in one direction . . . and I could change it.

So . . . perspective.

Then Brent had asked me out.

Officially.

And I was running with it.

I pulled in a breath then released it slowly, trying to imagine all the remaining, niggling doubts and worries being exhaled as easily as carbon dioxide. I deserved to be happy and right now, Brent made me happy. I was mentally editing out what would normally go through my brain in that moment: *for some reason*—because no, dammit, not *for some reason*, not because it was insane he was attracted to me, not even because of the whole he was gorgeous, and I was not thing.

I'd thought myself into a tiny compact ball, reduced everything good about me for way too long.

Now was the time to be kinder.

Now was the time for me to finally embrace that I deserved to find some happy.

Now was the time for me to go after something I wanted.

Today . . . that was Brent.

Tomorrow? Maybe it would be Brent covered in cherry pie filling as I slowly licked it off his body. I grinned at myself in the mirror then reached for my jacket just as the doorbell rang.

"You got this," I told the optimistic woman in the reflection.

The one that I almost didn't recognize.

The one I wanted to keep around anyway.

I MADE it down the stairs in record time, clomping in my chunky-heeled booties across the hardwood floor to tug open the door.

"Hi," I said, a little breathless from the jog to the front of the house, but mostly breathless because it was Brent . . . and *fuck* could the man wear a suit. It was deep navy with a bright white shirt underneath. No tie, which was a shame because the outfit definitely gave me the urge to take him by the tie and drag him into the next room. But the shirt wasn't buttoned all the way up, so I contented myself with fantasizing about caressing that triangle of exposed skin with my tongue . . . then maybe showing him how good my unbuttoning skills were as I made my way down.

I was good at shirt buttons.

But I thought I was even better at pants buttons.

Hadn't had a lot of experience with undoing belts, however . . .

Which was preciously the point—my gaze firmly locked on

said belt (which was in a killer shade of dark brown that also matched a cool pair of shoes that weren't old-man frumpy, but instead model-worthy)—that I realized I hadn't said anything aside from *Hi,* and that had been a good two minutes earlier.

I tore my eyes from the belt and brought them up to Brent's face.

Then realized he hadn't been speaking either.

Because his gaze was on me . . . or rather on my body. I shivered when it drifted slowly back up, almost as though he were tangibly tracing my curves, my skin prickling and goose bumps rising on its surface, my nipples hardening against the fabric of my bra.

And he saw my body's reaction.

Or, at least, I suspected it. Because my nipples got tingly and then his face changed, need sharpening his features as his eyes lingered there for a long moment before they eventually moved up to mine.

Heat.

Scalding brown eyes that threatened to set my body on fire.

He cleared his throat. "That's some dress, darlin'."

I nibbled my lip, started to murmur a "thanks," but suddenly I found myself in his arms, pulled flush against that broad chest of his, getting a close-up view of the heat in his gaze. "And then you had to go and bite that gorgeous mouth of yours," he said, a mix of velvet and gruff that slid over my skin, arrowing heat directly for my pussy. "I can't have you abusing this mouth." He brushed his thumb over my bottom lip, making my breath hitch. "Can I?"

If me abusing meant he'd hold me like this or hopefully *kiss* me like it was imminent based on his expression, then I was definitely going to keep the lip nibbling.

His palm slid up my side, fingertips drifting on the outside of my bottom ribs, skating along my arm, drifting up my throat before coming to a stop on my jaw. "Can I?" he asked again.

Cinnamon on his breath, glazing my lips like the most delicious frosting on Earth.

Calloused fingertips caressing my skin.

A hard chest against mine.

Our mouths perfectly aligned because of my heels.

Check. Check. Check—

I stopped cataloging, stopped thinking.

I closed the distance between our mouths.

Perfection. His lips on mine were utter perfection, and for one inane moment, I was glad I hadn't worn lipstick because I knew this was the kind of kiss that would obliterate the most carefully applied liner and stain. Especially when he managed to part my lips from one heartbeat to the next, his tongue sliding home, and reminding me why I'd lost a piece of my sanity under the mistletoe at Bobby's on Christmas Eve.

The man could *kiss*.

Gently coaxing one moment then his arms banding tight, pulling me even tighter against him as his lips and tongue demanded mine to meet him move for move.

Not a hardship.

Also, I wasn't just going to follow. I could lead, could be demanding, too. I slipped my tongue into his mouth, chasing his, nipping at *his* bottom lip. And Brent let me take the lead, at least for a moment.

Then he shifted, spinning us so my back was pressed to the open door.

My legs went around his waist, and he stiffened, lips coming off mine as he sucked in a breath that almost sounded pained, but before I could ask if he was okay, his palm dropped to my hips, angling my body, holding me to him so I could feel his hardened cock, just between my thighs. Then his mouth descended again, and Brent took control back, his mouth and hands working in tandem, frothing my desire into a tumult of need, until it felt like I might die if I didn't have this man inside me.

"Brent!" I gasped, throwing my head back when he slid his lips along my throat, nuzzled into the cowl neck of my dress, finding bare skin.

And . . . thank you, God, because his mouth closed over the hard bud of my nipple, suckling it through the fabric of my bra, the wet material and damp heat of his mouth nudging me closer to oblivion.

I moaned, tightened my legs on his hips, and gasped, "Inside!"

Without a word, he moved, lifting his hand and me from the door, slamming the wooden panel shut, and flicking the lock closed.

I'd meant inside *me*, right there, not giving a shit that we were making out in full view of anyone who might happen by. But I didn't have time to clarify that or even to complain he *wasn't* inside me because Brent slanted his mouth across mine, and it was very obvious who was in control.

That person being Brent.

He carried me across the room, dodging the box I'd intended to use to pack away another portion of Christmas Extravaganza, avoiding the coffee table, not disturbing the vases of ornaments on the sideboard, not doing anything except arrowing directly for the couch and setting me down on top of it.

But he didn't follow me to the plush gray cushions, didn't drop down onto me, pressing my back against them.

Instead, he dropped to his knees in *front* of me.

And this time, the coffee table was disturbed, shoved abruptly to the side, its contents rattling, a stack of blocks that spelled 'Merry Christmas' toppling to the floor, hitting the carpet with barely audible *thunks*.

My chest rose and fell in rapid succession as I struggled to suck air into my lungs, but any and all hope of that faded when Brent turned back from moving the table, and his scorching gaze met mine. "Darlin'?" he asked, no velvet left in his voice. Only gruff, and a gruff that sent all my nerves, but especially the ones between my thighs, tingling.

But . . . it was also Brent asking a question.

Brent checking to see if I was with him.

Well, I was about ten steps *ahead* of him. I wanted his hard cock—which I could see clearly outlined against the tight fabric of his slacks—and I wanted it inside me. I lifted a hand, reached for his belt.

He caught my wrist, lifted it to his mouth. "Behave," he murmured against my skin.

Not likely.

I was living my best life now, and that meant I was grabbing every opportunity—and okay, maybe the occasional hard cock, so long as that cock belonged to *this* man—to reach for what I wanted and deserved.

I lifted my other hand, managed to grasp onto the top of his belt.

But then Brent proved that he knew his way around a duck and weave. He snagged my other wrist, clasped them both in one hand, and shouldered his way in between my thighs.

Oh my.

I had Brent Collins between my thighs.

And it was glorious.

I stopped fighting his hold right about the time he let his free hand slide up the inside of my leg, stopping a hairsbreadth away from the damp silk of my underwear. I definitely stopped fighting when he slipped his fingers under the elastic and dipped them through my wet folds, unerringly finding my clit.

My head dropped to the back of the couch, my thighs instinctively spread farther, and a moan spilled from my lips.

Fucking yes.

"Up, darlin'," he murmured, helping me lift my hips so he could slide my panties down my thighs, over my heels, and off somewhere in the direction of my nutcrackers.

One hand returned, sliding up my calf, behind my knee, up my thigh, dipping back through my wet pussy. I expected to see his other hand reach for his belt, to finally release his cock, to finally, *finally* get inside me. But instead, he slipped both hands to my ass, lifted me slightly, and then bent, pressing his mouth to my center.

I screamed.

He paused, glanced up at my face, and his lips curved into a sexy smile that had more moisture drenching my pussy. Then that smile disappeared.

Because he dropped his head again, and this time he didn't stop when I screamed.

This time he kept going, tracing his tongue through my folds, drifting up to my clit and sucking firmly. I groaned, arching against him, pressing closer, my hands no longer reaching for his belt but gripping his head, angling him until he found . . . just . . . the . . . right . . . spot.

Teasing, flicking, zeroing in on what made my head spin, then exploiting what he learned, catapulting me up the edge of pleasure until I was on the razor's edge of exploding.

And then he slipped one large finger home.

I came apart against his mouth, clenching against the blunt intrusion, wave after wave after wave of bliss expanding out through my body, leaving me limp and sated and slumped back on the cushions.

I barely felt Brent remove his hands, was hardly aware of him tugging my dress down, but I *became* aware when he gently lifted me to my feet.

First, because how in the hell was I supposed to balance on heels—chunky or not—after he'd given me the orgasm to end all orgasms? Second, unless he was putting me on my feet so he could lead me to my bedroom then I was much more interested in being on my back on that couch than teetering on my heels.

He smoothed my dress over my hips, fixing the displaced collar, tugging down the hem over my panty-free bottom half.

Which—*hot*—was also not the point.

The dress should be coming up, being yanked over my head, not going down and covering up all the parts where I wanted his mouth and teeth and tongue . . . and cock.

"We'd better get to dinner, darlin'," he murmured, wrapping an arm around my waist.

Dinner?

Did sucking his cock off like a lollipop count as dinner?

Also, apparently living my best life meant transforming into a sex fiend—though I'd challenge any straight or bisexual woman to not become addicted to a man like Brent, especially when said man had just given me the orgasm to end all orgasms.

Yeah. I'd chosen the right time to start living.

Especially when Brent seemed to read my thoughts on my face, or maybe it was the fact that my eyes had dropped to his waist again, to the erection that was still present and pressing against the fabric of his pants.

"Trying to do the right thing, darlin'," he said. "Trying to show you a good time. Take you out for the nice meal you deserve." I leaned against him, knowing my breasts were pressed to his chest, knowing he could feel it, that he *liked* it because his breath caught, and his hands clenched into fists where they rested on my hips.

"Darlin'," he rasped again, warning this time in his tone. "We should leave now, or we'll miss our reservations."

I shifted in his hold, slipped my arms around his waist. "I don't care about reservations, baby." I lifted on tiptoe, my eyes staring into his. "I want you to take me in your arms and walk me down the hall to my bedroom. I want you to make love—"

"I can't."

I smiled. "I don't mean that you literally have to lift me. I know I'm heavy. But I want you Brent. I want to make you feel as good as you just made me feel. I want—"

"We should—"

I slipped my hand down, squeezed his cock.

"Fuck!" he grunted, fingers clenching on my hips.

"Let's go to the bedroom—"

"No!"

I blinked, horror washing through me. "Oh, my God," I said, jerking out of his hold. "I'm sorry. I'm so sorry! I didn't mean to make you uncomfortable. Oh my *God*," I repeated on a groan, turning away and shoving my hair out of my face, embarrassment coursing through me. He didn't want me. "I shouldn't have pushed. I—I didn't think. I—"

Warm hands gripped my shoulders, spun me to face him.

"I don't know what's going through your head, darlin'. But first of all, you're not too fucking heavy for me to carry, bad back or not," he growled, and before I could ask him about the bad back, since that was the first I'd heard of it, he took my hand and placed it over his erection. "And you're *not* pushing. Or not pushing me to do something I don't want. I *do* want you, baby. I just . . . we should take things slow."

I bit my lip, let my eyes drift away, feeling suddenly both unsure and also a bit like a hussy.

He wanted to take things slow, and I was the one trying to steal his virtue.

Cool.

And also, maybe I was all about living my best life and jumping in with both feet, but also . . . maybe Brent was just being nice. Maybe he'd realized he didn't want to hurt my feelings, but actually wasn't into me—

"Hey."

I shook my head and turned away again, searching for in what would prove to be a vain attempt for my underwear.

One, because I couldn't spot them straight away.

Two, because almost as quickly as I'd turned around, I found myself spun back to face Brent again.

"Darlin'."

Another shake of my head, my eyes burning. "We should just go to dinner, like you said," I blurted.

"I *do* want you, Iris."

Maybe more level-headed and clear-minded I would have recognized the angst in his tone, the insecurity, but I was heading down the road to a full-blown burned my pecan, cherry, *and* pumpkin pies meltdown and wasn't capable of discerning anything aside from my burning humiliation at coming on to someone who didn't want me.

Did that make me an asshole?

Probably.

Especially because my first thought to him saying he wanted me was, *Yeah, sure he did* and then trying and failing to pull out of his grip, because I'd just told the man who'd turned me down that we should go to dinner, and the horror coursing through me at the thought of actually having to sit across a table from him after knowing that he didn't want me, that I was a disgusting, pressuring asshole who couldn't read the signs was overwhelming—

Brent's face came very close to mine, fury crashing across

his features. "Fuck. S*top it*, darlin'," he snapped. "I fucking want you, more than I've *ever* wanted *anyone*—"

"Then why?" I snapped right back. "I don't want slow or careful. I want—"

"I'm a virgin."

My words died on my tongue.

Asshole? Yup.

Because I certainly hadn't seen that plot twist coming.

NINE

Brent

"FUCK ME," I muttered, dropping my arms and striding away from her.

"That's what I'm trying to do," she said, and I spun back, mouth falling open in surprise. She was going to make a joke about the giant bombshell I just dropped? But then she got a glimpse of my face, and her own mouth fell open. "Oh my God, Brent, you're serious?"

I nodded stiffly.

And cue silence.

Shit. It wasn't like I'd planned on being a virgin this long, but things happened and life got away from me, and all of a sudden, I was thirty-three and had done everything except actual sex.

A real catch, that was me.

"B-but—" Her eyes drifted to mine then away then back to mine, her mouth opening and closing like a fish. Eventually she closed her jaw, sucked in a huge breath, released it, then asked, "*How?*"

And more silence.

"How'd I get to be a thirty-three-year-old virgin?" I asked into the stunned quiet.

Iris nodded. "Um . . . *yes?*"

I bolstered myself for her to laugh my ass out of her house then gave her the TL;DR, otherwise known as the very glossed-over breakdown of my past.

"Grew up in a very religious family, so it was never on the table, never something I even thought about. I wasn't allowed to be alone with a girl, let alone have a girlfriend." A shrug. "When I enlisted and eventually *did* get a girlfriend, she was also from my church, and we never made it that far—mainly because we were both still really into the religion thing and then later because of a good friend of ours knocked a chick up and she was a total nightmare."

I sighed when her face remained shocked.

"So, anyway, we decided to wait. I was deployed, she got tired of waiting, and I nursed my broken heart for a good long while. Got close again, a few times, but the situation wasn't right. Then was deployed again. Hurt my back badly, my best friend was killed, and I was fucked up for a while—physically and mentally."

She made a pained sound and my eyes met hers briefly, just long enough to ascertain that the sound wasn't pity. Sympathy I could handle. Pity, not so much.

"Then I got better, started working at Bobby's . . . and you strolled into the bar and took my breath away."

Silence. Long, *painful* silence.

Then, "Oh."

Just *Oh.*

For fuck's sake, I'd bared my heart, and all I'd gotten in return was *Oh?*

Christ.

I started to look away, but my gaze was drawn back when she grasped my hand and squeezed lightly. "I'm so sorry about your friend."

"He was Brooke's brother."

She sucked in a breath, eyes glistening with tears. "Oh, no." She closed the distance between us, cupped my face in both of hers. "Brent. God. I'm so sorry."

"He wasn't the only person I lost there," I said, eyes focused on a spot over her head.

"Brent."

Just my name. Just that one word filled with so much pity, and I couldn't hack it.

"I gotta go."

"Brent, honey."

"I need to go, darlin'."

"I—"

Not letting her finish whatever she was going to say, I brushed her hands away then dodged her when she made to reach for me again.

Can't do this. Can't. Not right. Not good enough. Not—

The mental spiral continued as I reached the door, as I fumbled with the lock, kept blaring in the background so I barely felt Iris come up behind me, not until I'd finally managed to flip the bolt and grasp the knob, my fingers shaking like I had the world's worst case of withdrawals, and her hand dropped to my arm.

"Brent."

"Darlin'," I warned.

"I'm an asshole."

"I need to go." I twisted away from her hold, yanked open the door.

"I shouldn't have made that joke about—"

"No. It was what any sane woman would say when that much was dropped on her on a first date," I said, somehow managing to keep the words level, even though the *Can't. Not right. Not good enough.* mantra continued to pound in my ears. I took the stairs at a near sprint, felt my back seize in a way it hadn't in more than a year, but I pushed through the pain and continued hauling ass to my car.

Especially when I heard heels clicking along the concrete behind me.

I yanked at my car door and threw myself inside.

More pain, shooting down my spine, burning through my right leg, just like it had for months after I'd first been injured.

Fucking deserved it, too. Deserved to feel this shitty.

Couldn't save my men.

Couldn't save my best friend.

Didn't even know how to please a woman.

Except, Iris had seemed pretty pleased on the couch, hadn't she?

"Fucking hell," I muttered, pushing the button to start my car, deliberately not looking when the knocking came on my window, when the slightly muffled, "Brent. Wait," penetrated the glass.

I needed to get the fuck out. I'd needed to leave ten minutes before. Fuck, ten *days* before. If I'd never started down this path, then I could have saved myself this pain.

Another knock.

More of me deliberately keeping my gaze forward.

I reached for the gear shift, put the engine in drive, and got the fuck out of there.

I made the mistake of looking in the rearview just before I turned the corner, and seeing Iris there on the sidewalk, looking so fucking gorgeous in that sexy dress, those heels I wanted her to wear as I plunged into her wet heat, just made the hurts that had escaped the Pandora's Box in my heart sting even more.

Failure.

Not good.

Absolutely undeserving of anything that special.

I forced my gaze forward, concentrating with every ounce of my being on driving safely home. It was far from easy, especially with the pain lancing through my skull.

But I made it, parked, and was able to stumble up the few steps to my rental.

Inside the door, I dropped to the floor, resting my head back against the wooden panel, letting my eyes slide closed. Everything hurt, but I couldn't discern if it was from my back spasming, my old injury flaring to life, or if it felt like I'd just ripped my heart out, offering it up to Iris, and realizing as I held the beating organ in my hand, that it was wholly unworthy of her.

Dramatic.

Still, I expected to find a gaping hole in my chest when I glanced down.

When I didn't, I slid forward, stretching out flat on the floor to ease the strain on my back muscles and stared up at the ceiling.

My cell buzzed.

Or rather, it *had* been buzzing pretty much constantly since I drove away from Iris's curb.

I painfully extracted it from my pocket, lifted it up to my face and glanced at the screen. It was loaded with texts from Iris.

Fucking hell.

A few swipes and taps had her number blocked, had the texts deleted.

It was better that way. A clean state. Over and done.

Except as I dropped my phone next to me and closed my eyes, riding out the muscle spasms, I couldn't help but wonder if that was what I wanted.

Then I remembered that the world had shown me often enough that what I wanted didn't matter in the least.

"Hey, Kace," I said into my boss's voicemail early the next morning. "I hate to bail on you, but I seriously tweaked my back. I won't be able to make it in tonight. Sorry, man."

The words weren't enough to actually encompass all that I was feeling.

But they did enough.

He knew about my injury, wouldn't question it.

Which was good because my back *was* hurting. It was just that the hurt was minimal when compared to everything else—my neck was stiff and I could barely turn it side-to-side, my right leg was riddled with knots, my shoulder throbbed along with my pulse, and the muscles in my back were so tightly contracted that just pushing out of bed to take a piss that morning had been agony.

And that said nothing of making it to my bed the night before.

Or the way my insides felt flayed open and exposed to the elements.

"Fuck," I said, still unable to believe that I'd told Iris what I had, but also that telling her had stirred up so much shit in my soul. I'd convinced myself that I wasn't ashamed of being a virgin, that I didn't have *anything* to be ashamed about, and yet . . . I felt shame.

I was thirty-three. I'd served two tours in Afghanistan, had shot and killed people, had survived a blast that killed my friends, including my best friend, who'd survived the explosion, but had been irrevocably changed and ultimately lost his battle with PTSD. I'd managed to relearn how to walk when that hadn't been guaranteed, worked a job where I stood on my feet, where I lifted heavy shit, where I reached and bent and stretched—all of which had definitely been things my doctors had told me I'd probably never be able to do again.

And it all came down to sticking my dick in someone's vagina.

Pathetic.

I meant *me*. Not the fact that I hadn't slept with anyone, that life had dealt me some blows and tricky circumstances and it just hadn't happened. It wasn't even a religious requirement any longer, since I was no longer a parishioner in my parent's church. In fact, I hadn't been for years. Not since I left my small town in Alabama for two years in the middle Middle East, not since I'd seen too much shit to think of the world in such black and white terms then had returned home to have my heart shredded and my parents pass away within a month of one another.

A lot of the comfort of religion disappeared when I couldn't find the answer to why bad shit happened to good people, or at least, not something more than *God has a plan.*

I couldn't.

It hurt too much, and I'd left that part of my life behind when I'd returned for my second tour.

Then the deaths. My injury.

And still when it came down to it, I was embarrassed that I hadn't had sex. I almost wished it was something I was holding on to, something I viewed as precious, as valuable, rather than something I just wanted to be done with.

But instead of valuable, it was just this heavy ass burden I was desperate to be rid of.

"That's what I'm trying to do."

Fuck, Iris had looked so playful then, so expectant that I was teasing her, but all too quickly the horror had come, and then the pity.

I'd spent too long in the V.A. tolerating help and pity to deal with more, especially about something that concerned my sex life. And yet, I wasn't pissed at her. I was pissed at myself, pissed that I'd reacted like it was a shameful secret and then pissed that I hadn't been able to hold it together for a date before finding a way out of there with my dignity intact.

Instead—

"Ugh!" I groaned. "Enough."

I couldn't keep going in these mental circles.

It was clearly over with Iris. She'd been horrified, rightfully since I'd all but shouted my truth at her. She'd looked on me with pity and clearly didn't want to take on a thirty-three-year-old virgin.

That was fine.

It would be fine.

"Definitely fine," I said, carefully shifting in bed so I could put my pillow over my face. Maybe I'd accidentally asphyxiate myself with excess carbon dioxide and I'd forget all that I'd told Iris. Maybe I could pretend I dreamed it and then think up something better than screaming, "I'm a virgin!" thirty seconds after she'd come on my tongue.

Maybe—

I fell asleep to a constant, repeating pattern of maybes circling through my mind.

But none of those maybes brought me any closer to dispelling the tornado of shame swirling there, of ridding myself of the tenterhooks of my past, my failures, my hopes for the present and future. Because they'd all collided into something that just wouldn't pan out.

I'd known that.

I'd yearned for a partner, had hoped it could be Iris because she was incredible.

But that wasn't to be.

It *couldn't* be.

TEN

Iris

SO, it turned out that searching my family room for my under-wear was a uniquely embarrassing experience.

"Though," I muttered, tugging my purse strap over my shoulder and girding my loins. "Not as embarrassing as revealing something to the person you were dating, the one you were supposedly building some sort of a meaningful relation-ship with, and having said person laugh in your face and make a tactless comment."

So. Fucking. Terrible.

That terrible being me as a person.

I'd texted Brent no less than twenty times, had called him at least a half dozen, and I probably would have kept on texting and calling and pestering if not for the fact that midnight had come and gone. I'd already been an asshole. I didn't need to keep bugging him into the wee hours of the night.

So, I'd called off the cellular assault, had put on my rattiest sweats and a holey sweatshirt, and I had baked into said wee hours.

Which meant I'd had a good start on orders before I even headed to work.

It also meant that I had baked a giant platter of brownies in a pathetic attempt at an apology. Bribery, causing a sugar crash, I was willing to take any and all steps if it might mean that Brent would just hear out my apology.

I didn't even have grandiose plans of him giving me another shot.

I'd been a total ass and didn't deserve another shot.

But *he* deserved an apology.

Which was why I was carting my platter of brownies down the sidewalk to Bobby's, already dreading the conversation that was going to take place, but knowing it had to anyway. I also knew that this was probably going to be the beginning of the end of my time in the cool bar and that my proffered advanced copies of Brooke's books were certainly going to be rescinded.

Well-deserved.

God, I wasn't used to being the asshole.

That was Frank's job.

I'd paused outside the door to Bobby's, feet halting even as the self-flagellating continued, but because I was lost in thought, I didn't see Brooke until she was almost on top of me.

"Oh!" I jumped, nearly upending the platter.

"Hey, Iris," she said, smiling with her backpack hanging on one shoulder. "You coming in to hang out?"

"I . . ."

I didn't get to finish my sentence because the door opened in front of me, and I had to dance back, had to act fast to keep the platter of goodies safe.

"Shit, sorry," Kace muttered, taking it from me and holding the door for both Brooke and me to enter. "Didn't see you there."

"Probably shouldn't have been standing behind the door," I said.

Kace smiled at me. "I probably should look before throwing them open."

"Yo!"

Kace and I glanced up, or rather over at Brooke, who was tapping her foot impatiently.

"Yeah, baby?" Kace asked, closing the distance between him and his woman, slipping an arm around her waist and tugging her close. "Is that jealousy I hear in your tone?"

I snorted, the idea was so preposterous. Not only was Brooke fucking gorgeous, but Kace was madly in love with her.

"No," Brooke said and glanced around Kace to smile at me. "No offense, Iris. It's just that I trust my man." A light punch to Kace's arm. "But mostly, I'm impatient because that looks like chocolate underneath that plastic wrap, and now that I've had some of Iris's delicious baked goods, I'm not going to pass up another chance."

"Brownies," I said in confirmation. "Double chocolate fudge with peanut butter swirls."

Brooke moaned and extended her arms in supplication. "Thank you, oh gracious and kind Baking Goddess. I needed something fattening and filled with chocolate to get me through these edits." She made a grab for the platter, which Kace lifted slightly so it was out of reach. "And anyway, I think that Brent would have something to say about that, if I was jealous. Which I'm not. Especially when I just need choc—"

"Brent's not in," Kace said, brushing his lips across Brooke's before glancing over at me and lifting a brow. "Hurt his back last night, apparently?"

I bit my lip, nodded.

He'd hurt more than his back.

Fuck, I needed to get out of here. I patted my pockets like my phone was ringing. "Oh," I said, lying through my teeth when I glanced at the screen. "That's my employee calling. Go ahead with the brownies. I'll join you so long as he hasn't caught anything on fire."

Brooke laughed.

Kace's other brow lifted.

I turned deliberately to the door, putting my cell to my ear, and saying, "Hello?" to absolutely no one as I pushed out through it. I kept the charade up as I moved past the windows. Then I dropped it, right along with dropping the hope I'd been clinging to that I could make things right.

"I'M DOING THIS," I muttered. "I'm doing this because it's the right thing to do and he deserves an apology. So, suck it up, Iris Hannigan."

I was outside the door at Bobby's again, another platter of baked goods—snickerdoodles—in my hands, though this time, I'd carefully kept out of reach of the door's swing.

See? I learned.

Part of me couldn't believe I was here. I'd spent most of my walk home the previous day, most of the morning at work, continuing to reprimand myself for being a jerk.

But around two in the afternoon, I'd realized I needed to stop.

No, I hadn't done the right thing.

No, I hadn't handled myself properly, any more than I'd handled Brent's feelings with care. But . . . I'd made a mistake. I'd thought he was joking and misread the situation, which was clearly a sensitive, triggering issue for him.

I'd done wrong.

So, I needed to make it right.

First step of that was snickerdoodles. I made a lot of good things, but I thought that perhaps, my snickerdoodles were the best of all. Slightly crunchy edges, fluffy center, perfectly even coating of cinnamon and sugar.

They were the ideal olive branch.

Perhaps even more so than brownies.

"Right," I said with a firm nod, shifting my burden and pulling open the door.

I slipped through the front room, usually filled with boisterous college-aged co-eds, heading for the space in the back. The quieter, chill hangout space I'd stumbled upon during my first visit was where Brooke had her spot, where Kace and Brent worked the bar.

It was nearly seven, and I slipped through the opening into the back, quickly spotting Kace and the tats swirling over his forearms. He was leaning over the bar, and I watched as he deposited a soda on a coaster next to Brooke then a kiss on the top of her head.

She barely noticed, her fingers were moving so rapidly on her keyboard, and I hesitated just a few feet into the room, not wanting to interrupt her flow.

Instead, I shifted to Brent's end of the bar, eyes searching and . . . not finding him. Rather than seeing my sexy, Idris Elba look-alike with the smile that made my knees melt and my heart skip a beat, a tiny and I meant *tiny* woman stood in his spot. She was maybe five feet, and that was a definite *maybe*, but I could feel her confidence even from across the bar.

Small but mighty.

She glanced up, saw me, smiled, and set down the rack of glasses that I knew were heavy enough to strain even the muscles of Brent and Kace. But she didn't look strained, not in the least. In fact, she looked utterly self-assured in a way that was envious. She came over. "Need something to drink?"

Shit.

"Oh—I'm—no—I'm—" I shook my head, sucked in a breath, and tried again. "Sorry. I'm actually just looking for Brent."

Curiosity in her dark brown eyes. "He's not in tonight."

Was his back still bothering him? Or was he avoiding me?

Probably both.

"Oh." I mean, I knew that. He wasn't there, and she was working his side. "I just—"

"Anabelle, this is Iris," Kace said. "She and Brent are dating. Anything she wants to drink is on the house."

"No, I couldn't—"

"Got it," Anabelle said. "Nice to meet you. What are you drinking?"

"I—um—"

Kace's head tilted to the side. "You good?"

"Yeah, I haven't talked to Brent today, didn't realize his back was still hurting." Not a lie. Not a lie. "I should go . . . um . . . check on him?"

Yes, I was having trouble forming sentences. Yes, I'd said the last phrased like a question. No, I wasn't above beating a hasty retreat to save face at this juncture. Which was better than the alternative. Namely, me blurting out that I wasn't dating Brent because I was a giant screw-up and—

Go.

I spun then realized I might as well leave the cookies, because if I didn't, I would probably eat them all and end up too big for my clothes.

And still feeling like an asshole.

"Here," I blurted, shoving the platter onto the bar. "Snicker-doodles. Enjoy."

Then I spun again, starting toward the exit.

"Brent chose a strange one," I heard Anabelle say. "A good one, I think, based on the sheer volume of baked goods on this plate, but still a strange one."

"If she keeps bringing cookies like these, she can be as strange as she wants," Kace said, and at the door to the hall, I peeked over my shoulder to see he had already peeled back the plastic wrap and was shoving snickerdoodles in his mouth like it was his last day on Earth.

A group of giggling women pushed past me at that moment, one declaring in a loud voice, "Heather, you will *not* get me drunk tonight. I have to go home and—"

"Do Colin!" another woman in the group interjected.

They began cackling, continuing to tease the first woman, so I couldn't hear what Anabelle said in response to Kace.

But I did see her reach for a cookie.

They couldn't fix everything, but apparently, they could help people look beyond my strangeness.

I'd chalk that up to success.

Mostly because I didn't have anything else going for me.

———

Two more days went by.

Two days of me showing up at the bar with baked goods—cinnamon rolls and chocolate custard hand pies.

Two more days of no Brent in sight.

At least I was able to play off my disappointment when I strode into the back room, determined that this time I would make good on my apology. That this time I would see him and make things right.

But he wasn't there.

Though each time, Anabelle was, and it turned out, I was

right. She *was* confident. And funny, with a quick wit that I couldn't begin to match, but one that somehow didn't make me feel dumb.

Instead, she mostly had me laughing like a loon.

Which was a good thing, because I was feeling more guilty and miserable as the week went on. I knew Brent had the next two nights off, and because I didn't know where he lived but had been pretending, in the most oblique terms possible, that everything was fine between us, I couldn't exactly ask Kace for his address.

Kace probably couldn't give it to me anyway.

Employer-employee confidentiality. Was that even a thing?

"And then I told him that just because I'm Filipino doesn't mean I'm the resident expert on all things Asian," Anabella was saying, drawing my focus back to where it should be. On her and the conversation we were having during one of her spare moments.

"I thought all Asian countries were the same," I deadpanned.

Then panicked, thinking she hadn't gotten the fact that I was deadpanning and—

She chuckled and clapped a hand on my shoulder. "I like you, Iris. Even if you've never tasted Halo-halo before."

I grinned. "You promised to remedy that for me soon."

"And so I shall," Anabelle said, pushing off the bar and turning in the direction of a customer. "For a price."

"I'll make good on my end," I told her with a wave. I needed to go anyway, to keep up my charade of *Everything Is Fine in Brent and Iris World*.

But I didn't think my acting was very good. Kace was studying me closely, eyes unreadable, although the concern in his expression was easily discernible. I had two schools of thought on this matter. One, I'd be able to fix things with Brent, enough to convince everyone that we'd parted sort of amicably and I could occasionally spend my nights at Bobby's, slowly sipping on a glass of wine, laughing with Anabelle and with Brooke, when she wasn't on deadline.

Two, I'd never be able to fix it.

And Bobby's would be off the table.

I didn't want it off the table. I really liked being there, liked the atmosphere, the people, and how the space somehow felt like home, even when it was filled with strangers. It rounded out my existence since I'd moved, gave me another place that I could belong.

I really hoped I could find a way to keep it.

"Iris?"

I glanced over my shoulder, saw Kace had come up behind me.

"You good?"

"Great!" I chirped. "I just need to go . . . check on—"

"Brent?"

His tone told me he knew that wasn't true.

"Actually, no," I said. "I have dough rising at my kitchen for croissants. I need to put it in the fridge so it's ready for the morning."

That was true.

Although, it wasn't true that I had to do it strictly at that moment.

Still, Kace seemed to believe me because he just nodded, though those eyes stayed unreadable. "See you soon," he said. "Make sure you stop by in the next couple of days. I think Brooke will actually be done with her book and will be able to talk about whatever it is that put that look on your face."

"What?"

He tugged a strand of my hair. "Something's up. I won't push." A beat. "Unless you want me to?"

I shook my head.

"Okay. Talking with Brooke then."

I forced a smile. "Talking. With Brooke. Sounds great." I took a step toward the door. "I'll bring the baked goods."

"Don't need to buy friendship, sweetheart," Kace said then smiled. "But not saying they won't be devoured all the same."

"Right."

I nodded, tried not to think too hard about his words, at risk of crying, and fled.

IT WAS two in the morning.

I'd spent the evening being miserable and generally feeling sorry for myself. But now it was my witching hour, the time I always seemed to find myself awake, ruminating on everything I'd done wrong.

Tonight, I just couldn't do any more of that.

So, I pushed out of bed, slipped on my second oldest sweatshirt, and went down to my kitchen. I was going to make the hardest thing I could think of—my special-occasion-only, extremely-expensive-albeit-very-delicious nine-layer-cake.

Alternating layers of delicate chocolate sponge, each sandwiching four different fillings—ganache, homemade raspberry jam, crispy dark chocolate cookies and praline (both homemade then pulverized and stirred into a white chocolate mousse), and Bavarian cream whipped by hand, respectively.

It was riddled with technique-heavy ingredients and would take concentration.

So much so that I wouldn't be able to think of anything else.

Done. Good plan. Work your brain into submission.

"I'm trying," I muttered, stumbling into the kitchen and flicking on the lights, blinking for a moment against the brightness before I headed to my baking cabinet and began extracting the pans I'd need. And for the next forty-five minutes, I was distracted by the recipe. I'd gotten my ingredients out. I'd measured and prepped. I'd whipped up the batter for the sponge cake.

It was working. Sort of. Because if I could just keep my hands busy, my mind on the list of tasks ahead, I'd be okay, and I wouldn't feel so fucking ashamed anymore.

"Shit," I muttered, deliberately grabbing the carton of raspberries.

I'd just dumped them into the saucepan, along with sugar, water, and lemon zest when there was a knock at my door.

My first inclination was to be terrified that someone was knocking at my door at three in the morning.

My next was hope.

That it was Brent. That Kace had talked to him and—

I ran to the door, whipped it open, and found . . . Brooke.

"Oh," I said, my disappointment obvious. "It's you." I clamped a hand over my mouth, realizing how it sounded. "Shit. I'm sorry. I just—"

"I'm not the three a.m. visitor you wanted," Brooke said, matter-of-factly. "If I had Brent showing up at my doorstep on the regular, I'd be disappointed in me, too."

I stepped back so she could come in. "What are you doing here?"

She paused in my entryway.

More hand clamping, more realizing I still sounded like a jerk. "Not that it's not good to see you," I quickly added, the words slightly muffled from my fingers, "but . . ."

"It's three in the morning, and I'm showing up unannounced at your door?" Brooke asked.

Yeah. That.

She smiled, seeming to hear my unspoken answer.

"Kace and I were driving home from the bar. Brent had mentioned you lived in this house a bit ago, and we saw the light was on." A shrug. "I told Kace to drop me off and head home, though he decided to wait in the car."

I glanced behind me, finally noticing the car in the drive-way, Kace's form visible behind the wheel, or at least his face and hands via the screen of his cell.

"I won't take up too much of your time—"

The buzzer went, and I jolted. "I need to check on my—"

"Go," Brooke told me. "I'll grab the door."

With a nod, I hustled into the kitchen, stopped the timer, and pulled out the critical ingredient in my nine-layer cake.

The sponge was perfectly baked. Then I checked the pan I'd dumped the jam ingredients into. It was simmering away happily.

Phew.

But also simmering happily was Brooke.

I turned, blurted, "Want something to eat?"

Her eyes lit up. "Do you have any more of those snickerdoo-dles? Kace only saved me one, and I finished the sequel to Jace's book tonight."

"So clearly, you need something to celebrate," I said, pulling out my secret stash of cookies, because even though I liked to fit into my clothes, I liked sugary carbs even more. "When am I going to read it?" I asked when I'd grabbed us both mugs of milk and the cookies.

"The release date is later this year," she said, then did some blurting of her own, "So, want to tell me why both you and Brent are doing the self-punishment thing?"

I'd just bit into a cookie and nearly choked at her question.

"Um, what?" I asked when I'd managed to stop choking.

"I know I've been in the writing world this week, but I haven't missed the fact that you've been in the bar every night with goodies and that you're disappointed when Brent isn't there."

"I—"

"Further that," she said, talking right over me. "The stubborn man refused to let me or Kace check on him, which tells me that his back is actually bothering him, but since you're not blushing and didn't look remotely sexually satisfied when you came into the bar on Monday, I'd say that it didn't occur in some strange bedroom accident that I definitely would want to write into a book."

She paused to suck in a breath, and that break in her words would have been the perfect moment to tell her she was overstepping and to back off.

Instead, what came out when I opened my mouth was, "I *was* sexually satisfied." Because the orgasm that Brent had given me was fucking incredible.

Silence. Then, "Ah."

"It was just everything that came after it that was the problem."

"He panicked? Or you?"

"*I* was a jerk."

"Him," she said, almost to herself.

"No," I said, reaching across the table and taking her hand. "He confided in me, and I didn't handle it with the sensitivity I should have, and—" Fuck, now my eyes burned. "He ran off, and I've been calling him and trying to catch him so I could apologize and—" I broke off, swallowing hard.

"You blew it," Brooke murmured. "But you want to make it right."

I nodded. "Yeah."

"How much did you blow it?"

"I nuked it," I admitted.

"Well," she said. "And here I thought I had it all figured out. I thought he'd panicked because he hasn't cared about anyone in a long time, not since—" She broke off.

I met her eyes. "I'm sorry about your brother."

She smiled sadly. "Thank you." But then she inhaled and exhaled, and the sadness left her face. "I miss Hayden every day. I do. But I'm also at a point where I can remember the good times instead of feeling like my insides were sliced open when the memories pop up."

I wasn't sure what to say to that, so I just squeezed her hand lightly again.

"Brent isn't there yet," she murmured. "Which is why I thought what I did about the self-punishment thing. He still thinks he's responsible, just like I think you're still blaming yourself about your ex . . . at least, that's what my nosy self thinks."

I wanted to deny it, but Brooke wasn't wrong. "I feel like an idiot for not having seen the signs."

"I get that."

"But that and what happened with Brent are two separate things. I really messed up with him. I deserved to be punished."

"Punished how?" she asked carefully.

My breathing sped up at the quiet question, at the storm of emotions that had been brewing inside me for the last week, and finally, I couldn't keep it all in. "I deserve to be hurt because I hurt Brent. I deserve to have you and Kace be mad at me." I shook my head and dropped my eyes to the table. "I don't deserve a decent man in my life. I don't deserve to have all the goodness of Bobby's or the friendship we're building. I don't deserve advanced copies or a successful business or—"

I broke off as a tear slid down my cheek.

Brooke didn't say anything for a long moment.

Then, though her words were quiet, they still tore through

me. "Is that really you talking? Or is that some bullshit your ex planted in your head to make you think you're unworthy?"

"I—"

I faltered when the reality settled in.

Because I *didn't* know.

Was it me? Or was it left over from Frank?

And I really, really needed to know the answer to that question before I could expect to move forward in my life.

The timer I'd set for the jam dinged, and I jumped up, Brooke following suit.

"I know I've already butted into your life," she said, trailing me to the stove as I stirred the jam then transferred it into another container so it could cool quickly. "I know I've overstepped when we've just started being friends." A brush of her hand down my arm. "And I also know that while I definitely have night owl tendencies, I don't think you always do."

I didn't.

I was only up at this hour when I was unsettled.

When I'd worried about my business. After I'd found out about Frank. And now . . . because of Brent.

Brooke kept talking. "So, while I'm glad I checked on you and saw you were okay. I won't keep butting in," she said softly. "Just know that your ticket into my life, our friendship, isn't dependent on Brent. I love the man. He's as much of my brother as Hayden was." She tucked a strand of hair behind one ear. "But you, sweetie, you're great. All on your own. And I'm looking forward to knowing more of that greatness over many, many years of friendship. Brent, present or not." A beat. "Okay?"

I nodded. "Thanks, Brooke."

She hugged me. "I'll see myself out."

Another nod.

"Oh, Iris?" she asked from behind me.

"Yeah?" I was very deliberately spreading out the jam, trying not to feel rocked to the core but feeling that way anyway.

"My number is on the table."

I turned to see a piece of paper on the wooden top.

"And maybe something else you might find useful."

My brows drew down.

"Funny story," she said, smiling brightly at me. "Brent lives just three streets over."

I bit my lip. "Oh."

She took another step toward the front door. "And Iris?"

"Yeah?"

"I wouldn't mind being your taste-tester," she said. "Just in case the job opportunity comes up."

I smiled. "Is that your way of asking for a slice of my nine-layer cake?"

Brooke tapped her nose. "Got it in one." A pause. "Get some rest, sweetie. But before you do, make sure you program my number into your cell. You wouldn't want anything to happen to my number. Like the note getting lost or ruined or eaten by a squirrel or something."

I frowned at the sudden firmness of her tone.

"Okay?" she pressed.

I nodded, opening my mouth to ask about her obsession with me having her number when I lived two blocks away from where she spent nearly every night, but by then Brooke was already gone, leaving me holding the spoon and the dish holding the jam, and a bright white square of paper on my table.

I dropped the spoon in the sink, the jam in the freezer, then I walked over to the note.

My heart squeezed.

Because below her number was an address.

One that was exactly three streets over.

"Oh, Brooke," I said. "I really am lucky to call you a friend."

Almost as if she were answering that statement with an affirmation, I heard the front door slam, and a few seconds later, a car engine start up in my driveway.

Nine-layer cake.

Then I was taking a walk.

ELEVEN

Brent

"YOU HAVE A LOT OF NERVE, Brent Collins!"

I'd answered my door without looking, thinking it was the pizza I'd DoorDashed at three in the morning from the twenty-four-hour place for about ten times the cost of what a pizza during normal business hours would be.

Brooke stood on my porch, her hands on her hips, eyes flashing in anger.

"It's three in the morning—" I began.

"I don't care what time of day it is," she said, barging by me, her long red ponytail swinging as she went. My gaze drifted past her, to the SUV parked in the driveway. Kace lifted a hand but didn't move to corral his woman.

Then again, Brooke wasn't exactly corral-able when she was in a mood like this.

And no, I definitely would not be saying that aloud.

"What right do you have to put that lovely woman through torment for a week? She feels terrible and has been beating herself up—"

"I didn't *do* anything—"

Brooke talked right over me. "She hasn't been sleeping. She's been in the bar every night this week, bringing desserts for the staff, but any dumbass can see that she's looking for *your* dumbass, and you haven't come—"

"My back—"

"No!" she snapped. "I don't doubt that you hurt your back, but you know what doesn't hurt it? Speakerphone." She tossed her hands up. "Or voice text. Or fucking FaceTime!"

"Iris deserves better!" I shouted.

Brooke froze, teeth *clicking* together.

"She *fucking* deserves better," I said. "So, maybe I should have called or texted or fucking FaceTimed, but it was better that things ended now. Better for her to find out what kind of man I am now."

It hurt, and I missed her more than I should have, considering I knew her all of a few weeks, but it was better that things were over. Better she found out I was a fucking asshole now, better she move on and find someone worthy of her. And if that sounded like playing the martyr, maybe it was, but dammit, I was trying to do the right thing.

And that right thing was having a clean break.

Brooke's question was quiet. "What kind of man are you?"

I froze.

"Because the man I know," she said, and I heard the tears in her voice, "is honorable and kind. The man I know served this country and protected my brother to the extent that his body is forever changed. The man I know struggled his way back from the edge and then helped me away from mine." She released a shuddering breath. "So, why in the fuck does *that* man think that he doesn't deserve all of the happiness in the world?"

My chest rose and fell rapidly. I couldn't summon an

answer to that, because I didn't feel like the man she described. Not in the least.

"I think you *do* know that man," she said quietly. "I think you know that man is still inside of you, still longing for more, but I also think that the man in here"—she tapped my temple lightly—"I think he recognizes that even though what you have with Iris is new, it's also special."

I shook my head, not sure which part I was disagreeing with.

"I also think that man is scared."

My spine went ramrod straight.

"Because he knows she's special and if he allows himself to care, if *you* allow yourself to care for Iris, to love her, that you'll lose her, too."

Fuck. *Fuck.*

No. I couldn't be scared. I was trying to do the right thing by her, trying to—

Brooke stepped even closer. "Brent—"

I shook my head again.

"It's okay to be scared."

"No."

"You're allowed to feel this way."

"*No.*"

"That makes you normal—"

"I'm a virgin!" I all but shouted. "I'm a fucking virgin, so even if I wasn't a failure who couldn't keep the guys in my unit safe, even if I couldn't keep Hayden safe, even if I hadn't taken too fucking long to get my shit together to look after you, even if all of those things didn't happen, I'm still a fucking *virgin.*"

I'd rendered another woman silent.

I was starting to think that was my superpower.

Go me.

Brooke took my hand and tugged me toward the couch. I let

her take me over, let her pull me down and sit beside me. "There's a lot to unpack there, Brent."

I ran a hand over my hair. "Look, logically I get all of the things you said, and I get that what I said isn't logical because none of that is my fault and that it's not really a big deal that I'm a virgin."

"But?" She bumped my shoulder with hers, when I didn't fill in the blank. "Your silence tells me that *logic* isn't the problem."

Yeah, it wasn't.

"Okay, right. Since I'm just all about butting into everyone's life tonight, I'm going to keep on rolling." She straightened her shoulders, shook out her hands like she was a boxer getting ready to head into the ring. "Here goes. I know that I can't take away the pain of what happened, what you lost, what it was like over there. I get that it doesn't just magically disappear, just like the pain of losing Hayden never really goes away for me."

Hearing her say that made a spasm of pain slice through me, and Brooke saw it, putting her hands on my shoulders and pulling me in for a tight hug. "But, that right there, honey. You can't keep doing this to yourself." She jostled me lightly. "You can't keep punishing yourself because bad stuff happens." She leaned back, eyes fierce as they held mine. "It's wasting what Hayden gave up, what the others did, too. Because you have a life to live, and you need to make sure you don't squander it away."

I dropped my forehead to her shoulder, sighed.

"Iris is trying," Brooke murmured. "She feels like shit because she hurt you, because she's so used to being on the receiving end of someone hurting *her* that it's tearing her to shreds." She leaned back. "So, even if you think you two don't have a future—which would be a fucking *stupid* thing to think, but I also know I can't force you to make the right decision—she deserves to have the chance to apologize. I'm not saying you have to forgive her—"

"I already have."

And I *had*.

I also just hadn't realized it until that moment.

Because Brooke was right. I *was* running scared, terrified that I'd lose Iris, that I'd disappoint her, that I'd fail her, too, and because of it, I had grasped at the first thing I could use to push her away.

I glanced into the eyes of the girl I'd watched grow up and marveled for a second. "How did you get so smart, darlin'?" I asked, not bothering to disguise the wonder in my tone.

Her lips twitched. "I got really good at getting stupid, but someone"—she squeezed my shoulders—"someone set me straight a while back."

I pressed a kiss to her forehead. "Thanks for returning the favor."

"Does that mean you're going to talk to her?"

I nodded. "Talk, beg. I think I have both in my future."

She grinned then stifled a yawn and stood. "This is late, even for me."

I got to my feet and walked her to the door, but when I pulled it open, I found Kace on my front porch, eating my fucking expensive ass pizza.

Glaring, I marched over to him, snatching the box out of his hands.

"It's good," he said, through a full mouth, completely unconcerned. "In case you were wondering."

Huffing, I stomped back to my door.

"Enjoy," Kace called.

I grunted.

"Bye," Brooke called.

I smiled over at her, mouthed, "Thanks." And then I went

inside, locked my door, and flicked off the porch light. No more visitors.

Just me and my pizza.

And trying to figure out how I could possibly make up for what I'd done to Iris that week.

———

KNOCKING at my door woke me up.

By the bright sun shining through the uncovered windows, it was nearly noon, but it wasn't like I'd been sleeping well—not thanks to my nighttime visitor and definitely not thanks to the fact that I'd stayed up for a long time after Brooke had gone, puzzling through my feelings and trying to figure out how to stop myself from running scared again.

Because if I was going to do this, if I was going to talk with Iris, explain to her what happened, then she needed to know that I wouldn't do it again.

The knocking stopped and started again, not letting up for several minutes, and so with a groan, I dragged my sorry ass out from beneath the covers, even though it felt like I'd only gone to bed minutes before.

I stumbled across the floor, back stiff, though it was feeling better than it had in days. *I* felt better than I had in days.

Mostly, because Brooke had slapped some sense into me.

I stretched when I reached the bottom step, rolling my shoulders, tilting my head from side to side to ease the remaining stiffness in the muscles of my neck as I headed toward the door. If I hadn't been so tired, I might have learned from my lesson the night before, might have looked and seen who was standing on the other side of that wooden panel, might have glimpsed the bright blond hair through the window at its top, the peaches and cream skin, or maybe even the striking blue-green eyes.

But I was stretching, taking in the fact that my body finally felt like mine again, that my mind had followed suit, and so I opened the door without any consideration of who stood on my porch.

Or the fact that I was only wearing a pair of low-hung basketball shorts.

"I'm sorry!" Iris said, her words coming fast and furious, almost like she thought this might be her one chance to get it all out, so she was doing it as rapidly as possible. "I was a jerk and insensitive, and I didn't mean to make you feel small. I spent too long with someone who I allowed to make me feel like that, and I'm so ashamed that I made you feel that way." She inhaled, exhaled rapidly. "And it's my fault you hurt your back and couldn't work. I made you run off, and I made you feel bad about yourself, and I-I'm a g-giant asshole!" Her arms came up, and I realized she held a platter with a cake on it. She thrust the tray in my direction. "It's a nine-layer cake, and it's for you, and I'm sorry, and I'm going to leave now—"

Maybe it was the fact that I was tired.

Maybe it was the sheer onslaught of her blurted-out words.

Maybe it was just Iris.

Because I'd never had a chance of keeping my distance, and just seeing her in front of me, seeing her so upset that she'd wounded me, made it clear that the decision I'd come to just a couple of hours before was the right one.

I snatched the cake out of her hands, plunked it on the table I kept there for my keys.

It barely fit, but I wasn't thinking of that.

My mind was on Iris.

I needed her, needed her to know that this whole thing was my fault. "Darlin'—"

She launched herself into my arms, and I stumbled back, scrambling to keep hold of her while closing the door with one foot, flipping the lock and then letting my mouth come down onto hers. She opened immediately, tongue dancing with mine, lips softening, body melting as we kissed and kissed and kissed.

Finally, she pushed at my chest, and I pulled back, letting her have a moment to breathe. I was flying high on adrenaline and didn't think I'd ever need to breathe again.

Then she grimaced and I remembered morning breath. As in, my mouth was probably rank with it. "Shit, darlin'. Let me brush my teeth."

"What? No," she said. "I'm trying to apologize." Her fingers traced along the lines of his jaw. "Brent, I'm so sorry."

"Shh, darlin'. It's my fault," I said, trying to focus.

She shook her head. "No—"

I tugged her closer, slid my lips over her cheek, nipped at the corner of her mouth. Her tracing turned into stroking, fingers running over my pecs, and my mind fogged. Then she skimmed my nipples with her nails, making my cock pulse.

"It was my—" she began.

My hands fell to her waist, brought her pelvis flush against mine. Her breath caught, palms drifting down over my abs, fingertips slipping under the waistband of my shorts, and I felt the leash inside me snap. Without thinking of my back, I scooped her up into my arms, probably reversing my recovery by days, but not able to feel anything in that moment aside from her bare hands on my skin.

She didn't protest or squirm, just arched her neck so her lips could meet mine.

And then I was walking to my bedroom, dropping her onto the mattress, and I knew this was it. I wasn't letting this moment slip by.

She scooted up, resting her head on my pillow as my fingers

went to the zipper of the hoodie she was wearing. "Do you forgive me?" she asked, breath hitching when I yanked the garment down over her arms.

I'd momentarily lost the ability to speak, mainly because she wasn't wearing anything beneath that hoodie, aside from a see-through lace bra.

Peaches.

Her nipples were the orangey-pink of a peach and beaded, pressing against the lace, making my mouth water, my cock grow even harder.

"Brent?" she called, hands coming to my head. "Do you forgive me?" she asked again. "I need you to forgive me so—"

"Shh," I said, coming back into my brain, seeing the vulnerability on her face. "Yes, darlin'," I told her, knowing she needed to hear it, but also knowing she needed my apology, too. "Except there's nothing to forgive. This whole thing was my fault because of my hang-ups. I shouldn't have run off. I should have stayed and talked—"

Her mouth covered mine in a scalding kiss.

"It's my fault," she said when we broke apart for air. "I should have—"

"I know we're really good at blaming ourselves," I said, gently placing a finger over her lips. "But how about we both table the *should haves*," I said, "and instead, think about what we *can* have?"

She nibbled at the corner of her mouth, but her eyes went soft. "And what do you think we *can* have?"

"Everything," I murmured.

She smiled. "I like the sound of everything."

I kissed her then, and it *was* everything, the jagged pieces of my heart knitting together, the worry and disappointment and pain of my past easier to shoulder. Because she knew everything and still had come to me. I knew we had more to talk about, knew I still had far to go to make it up to her, but I also knew we needed a *can have* in that moment.

And I intended to give it to her.

I tugged off her shoes and socks, while she shoved down the waistband of her sweats, our hands tangling when I took over to slide them over her knees and off her feet.

Then she was in front of me, clad in see-through underwear, and I was suddenly very aware of the fact that I hadn't done this before.

"Here," she murmured, and my eyes flicked up to see she was stroking a finger across her lips. "Start here, and all the rest of it will fall into place."

Frustrated that I was inexperienced, that I was scrambling to stay in control and figure out what I should be doing, I blew out a breath. "Darlin'—"

Iris smiled, somehow understanding what was going through my mind. "I've done this with one other person, Brent," she said. "I'm not an expert by any means, but I do know I want you more than I've ever wanted anyone, that when you kiss me, the rest of the world disappears, and I can just . . . *feel*."

That.

That was what I felt, exactly what I felt and because of it, I didn't need any further coaxing.

I let my mouth drop to hers, allowed my hands to roam, and I stopped thinking. Because I might be a virgin, but I had done other things . . . lots of other things. My lips slid over her jaw, down her throat, along the tops of her breasts. I nudged the straps off her shoulders, baring those gorgeous peachy nipples, feeling my mouth water.

She moaned my name when I sucked one into my mouth, and since I really fucking liked hearing my name fall from her lips, I spent a while at her nipples, rolling one between my forefinger and thumb then suckling deeply at the other, alternating sides, sucking and nipping and loving the way her hands found my hair and gripped tight.

That sting on my scalp grounded me, pulled me back into focus when it felt like I would fall away.

Releasing her nipple with a soft *pop*, I traced my tongue over her ribs, drifting down, laving the dip of her belly button, tugging down her panties, and positioning myself at her center.

She spread her legs, eyes shadowed, lips parted, breaths coming rapidly.

"Pink and wet and glistening," I said roughly.

She choked then groaned. "Brent, get inside me, baby. Another time can be slow. I need you now."

The problem with that was I knew I probably wouldn't last long. Not only was I more turned on in that moment than I'd ever been in my life, but I'd never done this before, so I knew it wasn't going to take much to put me over the edge.

Which meant I needed Iris close.

I needed her so turned on and ready to fly that I wouldn't blow without her.

So, I ignored her reaching for me, ignored the plea, and knelt between her thighs. A heartbeat later, I had my mouth on her pussy, and it was the greatest fucking dessert in the world, sweet with an edge of tart and so damned wet that I could picture how that wet would feel on my cock.

I sucked her clit firmly, just as I'd learned she liked the other night, then circled her entrance and slid a finger home.

She arched up on the bed, head thrashing on the pillows. "Brent. Honey. I—"

I flicked my tongue, pressed the flat of it to her clit, and then alternated the pattern, driving her up until she was bucking against me, pleas tumbling from her lips.

Then I scrambled for my nightstand, for the package of condoms I'd bought before that first date.

I tore into it, yanked one out, then rolled it with trembling fingers down my cock.

"Now," Iris demanded.

And I didn't have it in me to tease or coax or ready bring her closer to the edge with me. I couldn't think, could only feel, and as I pushed inside her tight, wet, heat, I knew that I wasn't going to last long.

It was . . .

More than I could put into words.

Not just the sensations, because those were fucking incredible. But it was the connection. *Never* had I felt closer to someone in my life. Never. Not my friends. Not the people I'd dated. Not my first long-term girlfriend.

It wasn't this.

It was Iris, cheeks flushed, lips swollen from my kisses, her beautiful curvy body sprawled out beneath me. It was this woman looking at me with softness in those glazed eyes, her desire tempered with affection.

With love.

I loved her.

And that made this moment mean so much more.

I moved in and out slowly, wanting to prolong this time with her but knowing I wouldn't be able to for long, especially when she tilted her hips, arched farther, and reached a hand down between her legs to find her clit. "More, Brent. Please, *more*."

More.

Yeah. I could do that.

I picked up the pace, leaning down to kiss her, bracing myself on one hand as I pulled out and slid in, using the other to tease her nipples, to trace over her curves, then to tilt her hips when I found an angle that made her freeze, lips parting on a moan.

And I zeroed in, because the end for me was near, and I very much wanted her with me.

I kept at the angle, thrusting harder and faster, my free hand moving desperately, dragging her up the precipice with me . . . until finally, she broke, groan torn from her lips as her orgasm swept through her.

Thank fuck, because I was right there with her.

One more thrust and I was over the edge, pulsing inside her as my orgasm shot down my spine, and I came hard enough that I could have sworn I blacked out.

My forehead fell to her shoulder, breaths coming in rapid succession, my body dripping in sweat, and I said the only thing I could, "Well, darlin', now that I have an idea of what I'm doing, let's go for round two."

"What?" she gasped.

I lifted my head, heart light for the first time in ages. Because of this woman. Because I was taking Brooke's advice. No more squandering. I was all about living now.

"I love you," I said. "I know we have so much ground to cover, a lot to talk about, but I need you to know that I love you, Iris Hannigan."

Her face gentled, and her eyes filled with tears. "Honey."

"I'm so sorry I freaked out and left," I said, rolling us to the side and holding her close. "My head was so messed up, and I was scared that I already felt so much for you."

"Brent," she murmured, cupping my cheek. "I'm sorry, too. I should have—"

"No," I said, capturing her hand and pressing a kiss to her palm. "*I* should have—"

She nipped my bottom lip. "I thought we weren't doing *should haves*."

I nipped *her* bottom lip. "You started it."

"Did not."

"Did *too*."

I grinned.

She grinned, but then her blue-green eyes filled with tears. "How did I get so lucky to find you?" She sniffed. "I love you, Brent Collins."

I kissed away a tear that escaped, lightened my tone because I wanted her happy in my bed, not crying, and even though I understood her tears weren't from her being sad, I still liked those pretty blue-green eyes best when they were sparkling up at me. "Gave me the full name back, huh?"

Her brows drew together. "What?"

"I said, *I love you, Iris Hannigan,* and you had to give me the full Brent Collins back?"

She rolled her eyes. "You're not even making sense."

"You're always trying to one-up me."

"You're impossible."

"Well, *you*," I said and pressed a kiss to her nose, "make me think that anything is *possible*." A beat. "Plus, I got you to stop crying."

Iris sighed, shook her head. "Brent."

"What?"

"If you keep saying stuff like you've been saying, then the crying isn't going to stop, no matter how much you tease me."

I chuckled. "I love you, darlin'."

She sniffed, waved a hand in the direction of her face, and I saw a few tears had escaped. "This is *your* fault."

"Well," I said and flipped us over, positioning her on top of me, "since you're already crying, I may as well subject you to Round Two."

Her mouth fell open, but then she gave as good she got because she rolled to her side, tapped me on the shoulder, and said, "Well, rookie, you've got to take care of *that* first." She gestured to the condom. "Or *maybe*"—her lips came very close to my ear—"since I'm on birth control and I'm also clean—and I'm guessing you are, too—that maybe I might let you come inside me."

And just like that, hard.

And just like that, on my toes.

And just like that, all of my fears slipped away.

Because I had this woman in my life.

And I wasn't letting her go.

"Hey," I murmured, much, *much* later. "Want to hear a funny story?"

"Besides the fact that I still haven't regained feeling in my legs?" she asked drowsily. Round Two had been even more intense than Round One.

Which was saying something.

"*That*, I think, is far from funny," I said, nuzzling her throat. "*That*, I think, is the best compliment I've ever had."

"You mean the best compliment ever isn't me telling you that you pour a mean glass of Merlot?"

I grinned, lightly bit the spot where her shoulder met her neck, loving that when I did, she moaned softly and lifted her hand to rest on the back of my head, fingers digging in slightly. "Aside from that," I murmured against her skin.

"Then, is it too soon to say that I think you were messing with me when you said you were a virgin because that's how good you are?"

I laughed. "No," I said. "That's me mentally chalking that up into the Best Compliments Ever column."

"Then what's the funny story?" she asked lazily.

"This." I reached over her and pulled out the tiny package from my nightstand. Not a condom this time, I thought with a grin. But a tiny parcel I'd gone to three grocery stores at the butt crack of dawn to find.

Turned out, it was difficult to track down when it was after Christmas.

But I had, and I'd intended to bring it to Iris that very day.

Only she'd beat me to the punch by coming to me.

Why did I think that wouldn't be the first time it happened, her beating me to the punch?

I handed her the palm-sized package that I'd wrapped in cheerful Christmas paper—penguins wearing hats and skis as they made their way down a silver mountain top.

"What is it?" she asked.

"Really?" I dropped a kiss on her lips. "Just open it."

"Fine, fine," she grumbled, tearing at the corner gently. "You know," she said as she painstakingly pulled the tape free, "you gave me my only two Christmas presents this year."

Fucking hell.

This woman destroyed me.

"I love you," I murmured against her lips.

She smiled when I pulled back. "I love you, too." Then went back to work, slowly removing another piece of tape.

"Are you going to open that sometime this century?" I grumbled.

"I'm savoring it," she said, daintily working at one corner.

And then because I couldn't stand how slowly she was opening the present and also because I vowed to buy her so many presents the next year that she wouldn't even be able to count them all, I snatched the package from her hands, tore off the paper, and handed it back to her.

Her lips parted in surprise when she saw the sprig of mistletoe. "Oh."

"I know it's hardly anything," I said, thinking now that

maybe I should have spent my time buying her something that had cost more than two dollars in the clearance section.

She deserved diamonds and fancy trips and—

Iris launched herself into my arms, hooking her own around my neck and squeezing hard. "Thank you," she said. "It's perfect."

Then the tears came.

And I discovered I didn't mind her blue-green eyes filled with tears, after all.

Especially when I got to hold her tight when they came.

Then coax her into Round Three when they stopped.

We each had spent far too long not living our lives fully, and I vowed to make sure we would both grab on to every chance to make up for that lost time.

Later, after I'd had a huge slice of Iris's incredible nine-layer cake, I also realized I'd need many more Rounds in order to work off all the extra sweetness that was sure to fill my life.

But *that* was something I was wholly on board with.

EPILOGUE

PART ONE

Iris, One Year Later, Christmas Day

I WAS SWAYING to the music, singing along with the lyrics to *Have a Holly, Jolly Christmas* when I smelled it.

"Oh no!" I tossed the popcorn and cranberry garland I was stringing and sprinted into the kitchen.

Only to find black smoke pouring out of the oven.

"Shit!" I muttered, running over to it and snatching out the three full-sized pies.

Full-sized because I was hosting Christmas dinner for Kace, Brooke, Anabelle, Brent, and myself, and I'd decided that four full-sized pies were required, three of which were currently smoldering in the oven. One of which, the chocolate custard, was cooling in the fridge.

Just like last year.

And just like last year, I was destined to burn the shit out of my dessert.

"Dammit!" I cried, pulling out the pumpkin with a potholder and dumping it into the trash, then reaching in and pulling out the pecan and doing the same.

I couldn't believe it.

I knew I'd set a timer. I just *knew* it.

But the blackened pies would say otherwise.

Fuck. I had—my eyes flicked to the clock—twenty minutes until Brent got back from picking up Anabelle, who didn't have a car, and before Kace and Brooke showed up on my front porch.

And I was a baker who did not have enough desserts.

Again.

Well, I think I had some cookie dough in the freezer. I'd defrost that, throw together some Christmas cookies, and pair them with the chocolate custard. It would have to be enough.

But first, the cherry with its torched gingerbread cutout top would have to meet its fate in the trash can.

I pulled it out, carried it over—

"Wait!"

I glanced to the doorway, saw Brent and Anabelle. "It's trash, honey," I told him. "I burned them again."

Something flickered across his face, but I didn't have a chance to process it. Or at least I didn't until he snagged the pie from my hands, whipped off the burnt crust, and set it on the potholder on the counter.

Then I gasped and stomped my foot. "Brent Collins, you did *not* turn off my timer so that I'd burn the pies again and we could have cherry pie filling with vanilla ice cream again."

"Actually," Anabelle said. "That sounds amazing."

"Hush you," I snapped, pointing my finger at her. She hushed, though when I glanced up to offer an apology for snapping, she just grinned and said, "Keep going, I love hearing Brent get yelled at."

"Gee, thanks," the love of my life muttered.

I glared at him. "How *dare* you turn off my timer—"

"I didn't turn it off so that the pies would burn and we could have cherry pie with vanilla ice cream," he blurted, interrupting my scolding, but when I opened my mouth to say "what," he kept talking and my sentence never came, especially when *his* next sentence was, "I turned it off so that I could do *that*." And he pointed at the pie, sans gingerbread top, but plus one bright blue box perched amongst my hand-pitted cherries.

I gaped.

Then gaped further when he used the potholder to pick up the pie and dropped to one knee. "Iris Hannigan, my wonderful baking love who burns *all* the pies." I huffed, even though my lips were twitching, my eyes stinging with tears. "I love you, darlin', more than I ever thought I could love another person. You've given me my life back. No, you've given me a life better than I could ever imagine." A beat. "And five extra pounds to work off," he said and grinned.

I laughed.

Or maybe it was a sob.

I didn't know, couldn't be bothered to process it, not when the man I loved was down on one knee, holding up a cherry pie with a ring box plunked in its center, all while he was proposing to me!

"Will you marry me?"

"Yes!" I exclaimed then dropped to my knees, launched myself into his arms, and crushed my mouth to his.

It was only much later, after we'd come up for air, that I saw Kace had saved us from being splattered with hot cherry pie filling, snatching the pie from Brent's hands when it had teetered and nearly fallen, and setting it on the counter.

Brooke hugged me as Brent retrieved the ring, peeling away the plastic wrap he'd encased the box in. "We were hiding in the pantry," she whispered.

I gasped and swatted her arm. "And you let my pies burn?" I accused.

She grinned. "Brent had a plan." A beat. "Not one that made a lot of sense, but one that he was adamant about."

Brent wrapped an arm around my waist, tugged me against his chest. "It was a good plan."

I dashed a tear away when he slipped the ring on my finger. "Do you know how long I worked on that pastry?" I spun in his arms, eyes narrowed. Then I sighed and pressed a kiss to his lips. "But I love you so much for having that dumb ass plan anyway."

And because he was mine, because I *could*, I kissed him again.

At least until Anabelle made a gagging sound that had us breaking apart.

"Whose idea was it to have our family here for this anyway?" Brent muttered.

I touched his jaw. "Yours, and it was perfect." Then I blew out a breath, pulled out of Brent's arms and clapped my hands together. "Okay, who's hun . . . *gry?*" My question trailed off when I saw Kace, Anabelle, and Brooke gathered around the remains of my cherry pie, a carton of vanilla ice cream next to it, no bowls in sight, but spoons in hand.

Anabelle scooped a spoonful of vanilla ice cream from the carton and plunked it in her mouth then repeated the process with the pie. "It's delicious," she said, but it sounded a lot like "Shtsh shlishes," as she spoke around the bites.

"It's unsanitary!"

Kace shrugged. "Couldn't find bowls."

I plunked my hands on my hips. "But you could find spoons *and* the ice cream?"

"Yup." Brooke held up two more spoons. "Do you want in on this action?"

I smiled then felt my eyes burn with tears again when Brent whispered, "They're family, darlin'," in my ear.

"Not more tears," Anabelle groaned. "More *eating*."

I dashed one away, crossed to my friends, my *family*, and took a spoon. "Now *that* I can get behind."

Family.

Burnt cherry pie.

Vanilla ice cream.

A huge, sparkling ring.

Best. Christmas. Ever.

EPILOGUE

PART TWO

Anabelle

I SLIPPED out the front door of Iris's house, several containers of leftovers balanced in my hands, struggling to close it behind me.

The party was still going strong, but I had to head out. Though at least I was able to bring treats with me—albeit more of them than was polite. But I didn't have any shame. Iris had offered, and I was taking my stash to my car—the one I'd finally been able to afford to buy, in part because of the crew inside this little house.

My boss and owner of Bobby's, the bar where I worked, Kace.

My coworker, Brent, who was charming, even with the most annoying of customers.

Their women—Brooke and Iris. Though maybe more accurate would be to say that Kace and Brent were *their* men. Because those men no longer held their own hearts. They'd trusted them into Brooke and Iris's safekeeping.

It was great. I was happy for them.

But also . . . it wasn't for me.

I wasn't looking for a happy ending. I just wanted a safe place. I wanted to make a living and not rely on anyone else. I wanted to control my temper so I didn't dump a Cosmopolitan on the lap of a handsy customer and instead carefully dissuaded him from being an asshole.

Okay, that last one was a lie.

I definitely didn't mind dumping cocktails on handsy fucking customers, especially when those customers had an open tab I could charge said cocktail to.

I kind of liked being an asshole.

Just slightly less than I liked the crew inside. So, I wasn't looking for an exit, an escape from the love and the happily ever afters inside. Rather, I'd offered to go in and meet the alcohol delivery at Bobby's the next morning, to save the lovebirds from an early morning.

Which meant it was time for me to go.

I fumbled with the knob, shifting the containers to grab it then failing, then lifting a foot and trying to use *that* to close the door.

Newsflash. I wasn't a member of Cirque de Soleil and so it didn't work.

Sighing, I bent to place the containers down, something I should have just done in the first place.

Always trying to take the easy way out, Anna. Sometimes it's better to just take the hard one from the beginning.

"Thanks, Mom," I muttered under my breath.

Ten years gone and still chastising me from the wrong side of the grave.

Still never failed to make me smile.

She would like my friends.

"Don't."

I stopped mid-bend at the male voice.

"I've got it."

Tall. *Really* tall. Dark hair with a reddish tint. Olive skin. Bright blue eyes. And, *oh NBD*, maybe also the most handsome man I'd ever met.

I swallowed hard then frowned when he reached past me to close the door.

Then frowned harder when he rang the doorbell.

"Um," I began, wanting to ask him what in the ever-loving-fuck he was doing. But the doorbell had been rung and footsteps approached, and the wooden panel swung back open to reveal Brooke standing on the threshold, smile wide. "Did you forget something, An . . . a . . . *belle?*"

The smile faded from Brooke's face.

Her olive skin went pale.

Her eyes widened. Her eyes . . . that were the same shape as those of the man towering over me on the porch.

Kace came up behind her. "Everything okay—"

Brooke didn't answer him, just reached a hand out as though she expected to encounter a ghost, her voice shaking when she spoke.

"Hayden?"

ON THE ROCKS

On The Rocks is coming September 27th, 2020. Preorder your copy at www.books2read.com/OnTheRocksEF

LOVE AFTER MIDNIGHT

Rum and Notes

Virgin Daiquiri

On The Rocks

ALSO BY ELISE FABER

Blocked

Backhand

Boarding

Benched

Breakaway

Breakout

Checked

Coasting

Centered

Life Sucks Series (all stand alone)

Train Wreck

Hot Mess (August 3rd)

Roosevelt Ranch Series (all stand alone, series complete)

Disaster at Roosevelt Ranch

Heartbreak at Roosevelt Ranch

Collision at Roosevelt Ranch

Regret at Roosevelt Ranch

Desire at Roosevelt Ranch

Phoenix Series (read in order)

Phoenix Rising

Dark Phoenix

Phoenix Freed

Phoenix: LexTal Chronicles (rereleasing soon, stand alone, Phoenix world)

From Ashes

In Flames

To Smoke

KTS Series

Fire and Ice (Hurt Anthology, stand alone)

Stand Alones

Someday, Maybe (YA)

ABOUT THE AUTHOR

USA Today bestselling author, Elise Faber, loves chocolate, Star Wars, Harry Potter, and hockey (the order depending on the day and how well her team -- the Sharks! -- are playing). She and her husband also play as much hockey as they can squeeze into their schedules, so much so that their typical date night is spent on the ice. Elise changes her hair color more often than some people change their socks, loves sparkly things, and is the mom to two exuberant boys. She lives in Northern California. Connect with her in her Facebook group, the Fabinators or find more information about her books at www.elisefaber.com.

facebook.com/elisefaberauthor

amazon.com/author/elisefaber

bookbub.com/profile/elise-faber

instagram.com/elisefaber

goodreads.com/elisefaber

pinterest.com/elisefaberwrite